THE RELIC OF THE BLUE DRAGON

D1331882

CHILDREN OF THE DRAGON

THE RELIC OF THE BLUE DRAGON

REBECCA LIM

ALLEN&UNWIN
SYDNEY • MELBOURNE • AUCKLAND • LONDON

First published by Allen & Unwin in 2018

Allen & Unwin
83 Alexander Street
Crows Nest NSW 2065
Australia
Phone: (61 2) 8425 0100
Email: info@allenandunwin.com
Web: www.allenandunwin.com

 A catalogue record for this
book is available from the
National Library of Australia

ISBN 978 1 76029 736 7

For teaching resources, explore
www.allenandunwin.com/resources/for-teachers

Cover and text design by Sandra Nobes
Cover and chapter illustration by Geoff Kelly/Tou-Can Design
Other internal illustrations by Rebecca Lim
Set in 11½ pt Janson Text by Sandra Nobes
Printed in June 2018 by McPherson's Printing Group, Australia

10 9 8 7 6 5 4 3 2 1

To Michael, Oscar, Leni and Yve –
through thick and thin,
and all the stuff in between.

Chapter 1

Harley Spark, thirteen years and twenty days old, had never stolen anything in his life. Although Harley's dad, Ray, was a major (unconfirmed) underworld crime figure.

When Harley was five, police in full riot gear had stormed their house, looking for a collection of antique pistols Ray was supposed to have nicked from a museum in Belgium. Harley's mum, Delia, had stopped having anything to do with Ray after that because, in her own words, she was *very black and white on the whole lying and stealing thing.*

Before then, Delia had been under the impression that Ray was a removalist.

'Oh, he's a *removalist* all right,' the policemen had said darkly as they'd left the house, empty-handed.

Around Ray Spark, things had a tendency to go missing and then pop up somewhere else. Somewhere a very, very long way away. It was just that no one could ever prove it.

To Harley, though, his dad had always seemed like a perfectly normal dad. Harley and his mum lived across town from Ray now, but Harley still saw him at least once a month and on birthdays and alternate Christmases – alleged illegal activities permitting.

They did things like kick the footy around and go out for ice-cream and games of laser tag. They were like two peas in a pod except that Harley's eyes were a light, almost golden brown whereas his dad's were blue, and Harley's hair was black like his mum's while his dad's was sandy. Harley had the same cowlick in his fringe that his dad did, and he wrinkled his nose the exact same way when he sneezed.

'But other than that,' Delia would say with great satisfaction, 'you are one hundred and five per cent my decent, law-abiding boy.'

Except for today.

Today, Harley was having a moment. It was one of those moments he tried to shove down and not acknowledge; one of those moments when he seemed to take after his dad more than his mum.

There was this auction house, see, just two doors down from the skinny single-storey terrace Harley shared with his mother. Every Friday, Hammonds the Auctioneers would sell the old junk that people no longer wanted in their lives. All week, until Friday morning, the front windows of the auction house would grow progressively more crammed, from top to bottom, with bric-à-brac – otherwise known as *lesser objets d'art*, according to the huge sign in the window, which also invited people to consign '**YOUR CURIOS AND BIBELOTS, GOOD CASH PAID WITHIN FOURTEEN DAYS OF SETTLEMENT**'.

People would spill out onto the footpath early on Fridays, raising their hands for things like porcelain cats, soup bowls resembling large cabbages and lampstands in the shape of sexy ladies, until the front windows of Hammonds the Auctioneers were empty and dusty. Then it would all start again the following Monday: people bringing in their sad, unwanted things until the Friday, when other people took those same things off their hands, forever.

Every time Ray dropped Harley home in front of the auction house (so that Delia wouldn't spot him hanging around outside their terrace and begin to cry), Ray would note absently, 'There is *no* cash – by definition, son – that is ever *bad*. It's only ever good. Saying *good cash* is completely beside the point. It's *otiose*. Useless.'

But today – a Thursday – Harley was feeling *bad* – Ray Spark-style bad – the way cash wasn't, because Hammonds was crammed to the rafters with people's junk *except for this one dusty blue and white Chinese vase that was just sitting on the footpath outside.*

Right in Harley's way.

One of the big, hairy men who moved the bric-à-brac, *lesser objets d'art* and all the other curios and bibelots around must have forgotten to take it inside the shop.

Harley was well known to be an inveterate collector of fossils, like fossilised dinosaur poo. He knew about old stuff – *old stuff that mattered*. Which is another way of saying that he normally wouldn't be caught dead anywhere near old ornamental thingummies made for putting flowers in.

But somehow this particular old ornamental

vase thingummy was different. He couldn't take his eyes off it, even though it didn't look like much.

Now, Harley was on his way home from school.

He was literally just metres from his house.

It was freezing cold outside, and he was also kind of busting to go to the toilet.

Harley reminded himself sharply that he was *decent* and *law-abiding*.

But something made him crouch down and study the vase more closely anyway.

Before he knew it, he had picked it up and was scrubbing at the dull, grimy surface, all over, with the sleeve of his blue school jumper.

The vase wasn't very big or very heavy; it was maybe thirty centimetres high with one very long, azure-coloured Chinese dragon looped and coiled around and around the body and neck of the vase on a cracked white background.

The dragon was side-on, with its head tilted slightly towards him so that Harley could make out two golden, stag-like horns and two burning gold eyes with black centres ringed in a thin line of blue, which had such a lively, inquisitive expression that the painted dragon seemed almost alive. The dragon's four legs ended in talons kind of like an eagle's, though with five claws on each foot instead of four, and it had no wings. Its rippling, snake-like body had scales like a fish, and a large, almost translucent pearl was suspended beneath its jaws. Harley – staring hard at the coils of the beast – could have sworn that he saw them move, just for a moment, the way a wave at the beach might do on a sunny day.

The feeling – that he needed the vase, and the vase needed him back – exploded in Harley then. Maybe it was the kind of feeling Ray got when he saw something old and unique and impossible to own.

It was this feeling that he just *had to have it*.

Harley knew that the vase was calling out to him to be taken away. And in a hurry.

Now you and I and Harley know that stealing is wrong.

But something overcame him just then – like a rush of blood to the head – and he hoisted his schoolbag higher on his back, stuck the vase as far up under his school jumper as it would go, and sprinted the two doors home.

Harley's mum was a senior nurse in the emergency room of a big city hospital. It was one of the afternoons where she hadn't arrived home yet and, for once, Harley was glad to be on his own. It would be at least dinnertime before she made an appearance: plenty of time before that to put on the oven to heat up the pasta bake she'd left him, and come up with a decent hiding place for the vase.

Hot with a mix of shame and something suspiciously like excitement, possibly even outright joy, Harley reached his small bedroom at the rear of the house and pushed back the sprawl of books on fossils, fossil-related doodads (magnifying glasses, tweezers and the like) and *actual* fossils on his desk. Sinking into his swivelly desk chair, Harley put the dragon vase in the space he'd cleared, gobbling it up greedily with his eyes.

Now that Harley had rubbed the layer of dirt off the vase, the paint seemed so fresh that the dragon might have been painted yesterday. There were no words for a blue like the hue of the dragon which, when he stared harder, seemed to have veins of gold shot through it, too.

He turned the vase around in his hands, struggling to follow the many twisting loops and coils of the horned beast. It was strange, because every time he started at the head again, then worked his way down and around to the tail, the shape of the dragon seemed different, or the head appeared to be tilted a different way. One time, he imagined the dragon even closed one of its eyes briefly, as if it were winking at him.

Harley's head began to feel quite fuzzy with the effort of studying the dragon. It was as if the dragon were a strong magnet and his eyeballs were made of iron filings. Harley couldn't look away. He felt a small thrill of fear, and desperately wanted to put the vase down because he really was busting now. But he couldn't do it, or even get out of his chair. It was as if there were strong glue all over his hands, and on the seat of his grey school trousers.

The light through Harley's bedroom window began to fail. He'd lost track of how long he'd been there. When his mum, Delia, stuck her head of sleek black bobbed hair around the corner of the bedroom door, she was perturbed to find him sitting there, in the autumnal gloom, with no light on.

She'd been about to say crossly, 'Weren't you supposed to get tea started half an hour ago, Harls?'

But something about her son's frozen figure made her say instead, 'What have you got *there*?'

Harley didn't answer, and he didn't turn around. He continued to sit hunched over, his bent head and gaze focused intently on something in his hands.

Fear suddenly seized Delia tight, the way it had when Harley was five, and all the policemen in helmets and combat gear had stormed through the front and back doors simultaneously, screaming at them to *Get down! Get down!*

'What have you *done*, Harley Spark?'

Delia wasn't ordinarily a person to panic. As an emergency nurse she'd seen just about everything – living, breathing people with knives stuck in their heads or metal poles through their chests – but panic gripped her now. Harley sat on in the dark, facing away from her, as if he were made of stone.

She lunged forward across the room, spinning her son around in his chair.

Something in his sweaty, frozen face and glazed eyes made Delia scrabble and pull at the thing in his hands: a cracked, blue and white vase with some kind of snake-like creature on it with golden eyes.

But Harley hung on grimly as if his hands were made of something other than flesh and bone. Suddenly, they were like hands and fingers made of unbreakable diamond. No amount of yanking at the vase would make him release it.

'Help me!' Harley's voice was a tiny wisp of itself, his mouth barely moving.

He was super ticklish, everyone knew that, but even Delia going for his armpits, then the skin under his chin, couldn't produce a single reaction.

'*Mum!*' Harley's fearful cry was even more frightening because it was so tiny and hard to hear.

Under her hands, she felt Harley's skin start to go smooth and hard and rigid, as if he and the vase were somehow *fusing together*.

'I don't know how to help you!' Delia wailed.

'Break it.' His voice was barely audible now in the darkened room. It was like the sound two leaves might make, rubbing together in a breeze. Delia might have imagined it.

But she didn't hesitate. She picked up the giant fossilised *Cleoniceras* ammonite that Harley kept on a polished wooden stand on the right side of his desk – his most treasured possession apart from the special whizz-bang phone Ray had given him for his thirteenth birthday – and brought it down on the side of the vase in Harley's hands.

As the vase shattered into pieces, a bright, hot golden light filled the room, as did the sound of Harley's and his mum's terrified screams.

Chapter 2

The light was so bright that Delia and Harley, their arms tight around each other in terror, couldn't look into it. So they didn't see how the outline of a girl seemed to form in the brilliant glare emanating from the shards of the broken vase as if she were coming back together from a place very far away. Even when the light abruptly vanished and the room was left in darkness, mother and son were so dazzled for a long moment that they did not realise they were no longer the only people in the room.

When their sight finally cleared, Delia and Harley both gave a startled yell that made the girl in the belted tunic and floor-sweeping skirt flinch back. They could just make her out in the moonlight now streaming into Harley's bedroom. She was very much there – standing with the remains of the broken vase around her slippered feet – where she very much hadn't been before.

Moving very, very slowly, so as not to startle their visitor, Harley Spark reached sideways and turned on the green-shaded banker's lamp on his desk. The three of them stared at each other, wide-eyed.

The girl was thin, about the same height as Harley, and her straight black hair was severely parted down the centre, hanging to just below her narrow, bony shoulders. Her eyes were jet black apart from a thin ring of blue – the same azure blue of the vase – around each iris. And the whites of her eyes weren't actually white; they seemed the faintest bit *golden*, but it could have been the warm glow of Harley's desk lamp that made him think that. The girl's finely boned, long-fingered hands were held up like blades, thumbs tucked in tight against her palms, in a protective stance that Harley – the veteran of exactly three weeks of tae kwon do lessons – vaguely recognised as a good defensive position.

She had a triangular face with high, pronounced cheekbones and her wide mouth was set in a straight and angry line under thunderously drawn-together brows. The tunic she wore – plain black but crawling with the looping bodies of six coiled dragons embroidered in silk threads of azure and gold, the left lapel crossed tightly over the right – was the most beautiful garment Delia had ever laid eyes on. It had fluid bell-like sleeves and the hem of it ended almost halfway down the girl's A-line, floor-length skirt of gold. Even the girl's flat-soled black cloth slippers were embroidered, each with three sinuous azure and gold dragons winding across it. The tightly knotted wide cloth sash that held the lapels of the collarless tunic closed were weighted down at the ends with two C-shaped dragons carved out of a vibrant blue stone.

'I bet that's lapis lazuli,' Harley breathed, being an expert on cool old stuff that came out of the ground. He'd never seen the rare blue stone except inside a book.

Around her neck, on a simple ribbon, the girl wore a large, almost translucent pearl that rested in the hollow between her collarbones.

The girl shouted something at them then that Delia and Harley could never agree on, forever after. It was a phrase ending in a drawn-out hiss that immediately raised the fine hairs on the back of the Sparks' necks. The girl's words seemed to enter their eardrums almost painfully, the way the cold wind does on a winter's day when you're coasting down the hill towards home on your bike, and you've forgotten to wear a beanie.

Whatever she'd said had seemed to resonate, even *burn*, inside their minds. Harley watched his mum shake her head from side to side, as if to dislodge the sound.

Delia, whose Chinese great-great-great-great-grandfather had come over to Australia in a nineteenth-century gold rush, wondered if it was Chinese the girl was speaking. Delia had done one year of Chinese at university a long, long time ago, failing it miserably. She hadn't absorbed enough of it to remember, and she certainly couldn't recall the language involving any *hissing* quite like that. But her tattered hardcover English to Chinese, Chinese to English dictionary was still somewhere in the house and it was time to put it to good use. She held out her hand to the girl in a frantic *Wait here!* gesture, then dragged Harley out of his bedroom with her, leaving the young stranger standing there, looking astonished.

'Who *is* she?' Delia hissed over her shoulder.

Harley shrugged in honest bewilderment.

'Where is it? Where is it? Where is it?' Delia cried as she rummaged through the sagging bookcase in the poky dining room that doubled as a study. The bookcase held tomes on flower arranging and novelty cake baking interspersed with medical textbooks filled with horrible pictures of burns, infectious diseases and wound care, with a special emphasis on gangrene prevention. Harley could never look inside those ones without feeling like he wanted to chuck.

Delia's Chinese dictionary had been almost entirely useless to her because she'd bought a second-hand, early twentieth-century version that predated the mass simplification and standardisation of the entire written Chinese language. The characters inside the dictionary hadn't remotely resembled any of the ones she'd been studying at university and she'd never got around to buying the right dictionary despite all the nagging from her grandma (which meant she never picked up much of the language, in the end).

'But it could still be useful in this instance,' Delia huffed, almost to herself. After all, there was something distinctly unmodern and unstandardised about the way the girl looked. 'There it is.'

She pulled out a thick hardback book covered in a worn blood-red cloth, its spine sharing English and Chinese characters in faded gold. Delia ran from the dining room, Harley hard on her heels.

Delia flicked on the overhead light in Harley's bedroom and they both felt a chill when they saw that the room was now empty. The girl might have been a figment of their fevered imaginations – except for the pieces of broken pottery littering the scratched surface of the hardwood floor.

'What—' Harley began to say, but the air was suddenly rocked by the sound of a contained explosion. There was no other word for it. It had come from the front of the house.

Harley and his mum – still clutching the brick-like book – turned and sprinted back down the narrow hallway towards the front door. When they reached the sitting room and flicked on the light, they saw the girl standing a metre from the only TV they owned which now had a hole in it the size of a bowling ball, and was smoking gently. A horrible smell of burnt plastic wafted around the room.

Harley howled, 'You *killed* it!' Harley loved his TV almost as much as he loved his fossils and rocks.

The girl let her cupped hands fall easily to her sides, not looking in the least bit guilty or sheepish. She regarded the Sparks, peering at her through the open sitting room door, steadily.

Delia's look of horror began to soften as she saw the girl's eyes flick away from them to search the room intently – taking in the old electric sunburst clock on the wall, the calendar turned to the month of April, the chunky twenty-year-old stereo system on the sideboard, the magazine rack on the wall crammed with gossip magazines and old newspapers.

'I think she might have been trying to turn it on,' Delia murmured over Harley's groans of sheer disbelief. 'Here,' she said quickly, holding the dictionary out to the girl in the beautiful tunic and floor-sweeping skirt. 'Just point to what you want to say, all right?'

The girl did not recoil from the tome as Delia had half-expected her to, but considered it for a long moment before reaching out to take it. As she did so, a crack of static energy passed from the girl's fingertips to Delia's. Delia drew back, shocked, glancing at Harley, who'd seen it too: an instant of bright blue light.

Power, whispered the voice that lived in Harley's head; the same voice that had convinced him that taking the vase from the footpath outside Hammonds would be a good idea.

The girl paged furiously through the battered dictionary, her frown deepening as she sped down the columns of words and characters with her eyes and fingers as if she were drinking them all in but not liking what she saw. She reached the midway point of the book – where Chinese characters were highlighted in bold with an English definition next to them, rather than the other way around – and started to shake her head violently in clear distress, her poker-straight black hair falling about her face.

'It looks as if she's searching for something she … recognises,' Delia whispered.

'But it's all in Chinese. Isn't she Chinese?' Harley hissed back. 'She *looks* Chinese. I mean, she's dressed like a lady from an old kung fu movie. She's just missing those bun and chopstick things on her head. Why wouldn't she recognise any of the characters? Maybe she can't – read?'

'No,' Delia said absently, watching as the girl's finger stopped on a single character near the end of the old volume. 'I think she *can* read – but the language … maybe it's changed. A lot.'

In fact, Delia knew it *had* changed. Around 1949, to be precise – and maybe a thousand times before then. Something like awe was beginning to take hold of Delia, although she couldn't begin to put words around what was dawning in her brain because it seemed too fantastic and ridiculous to utter out loud. This was just a kid in fancy dress, right?

The girl stepped towards them, holding out the book still open under her finger, and Delia and Harley retreated automatically, remembering the spark of intense blue light that had passed between her and Delia. The girl jabbed impatiently at the page and Delia leant forward cautiously to look at the character highlighted there.

Delia smiled. It was one of the few characters she remembered from her disastrous year of Chinese study, because it looked exactly like what it was supposed to mean.

'It means *people*,' Delia murmured to Harley. 'See how those are supposed to be legs, walking?'

The girl made a circling gesture at Delia and Harley – as if she were throwing a lasso around them – then stamped the floor with a small, emphatic, slipper-shod foot. It was Harley's turn to make a *Wait here!* gesture as he raced into his bedroom to grab the plastic world globe someone had given him for his twelfth birthday.

He ran back into the sitting room with it and spun it on its axis under the girl's short, straight nose. Mirroring the encircling motion the girl had made, Harley pointed at the image of Australia at the base of the globe. When the girl tucked the dictionary under one arm and reached for it, Harley almost dropped the globe in alarm.

He made sure that their hands did not touch as the girl placed the stand in one palm and slowly rotated the globe with the other, pausing as her gaze fell on the large landmass at the top of the world with *CHINA* printed across it. Her face seemed to clear a little.

Delia nodded. 'Yes?' she said eagerly, putting her two thumbs up and grinning like a maniac.

The girl looked at Delia's upraised thumbs

blankly, then held out the globe to Harley, who shook his head and flapped his hands at her nervously, indicating she could keep it.

Giving him a faintly reproachful look, the girl put the globe on the floor at her feet and paged back through the dictionary until she stopped again and held it out to them.

'Ooh,' said Delia, perturbed. 'I *know* that one, but I always mixed it up with the characters for *eye* and *white* because they all looked so similar. What *is* that? It's one of the three hundred most common characters. You could say I wasn't a natural at the Chinese language, Harls. Though Chinese food is a whole different story.'

'May I?' Harley said, indicating the dictionary in the girl's hand.

She handed it over quickly, zapping him in the process so that he cried out. Glaring at the girl with a wounded expression – because he actually *was* wounded – Harley read the definition out loud. 'It means *day* or *sun.*'

Delia stared at the girl for a moment. 'She wants to know who we are,' she whispered. 'As in, what manner of people are *we*? And she wants to know what … day it is.'

'*When* it is,' Harley interjected in sudden understanding. 'But I can't believe in all that great big book of Chinese she's only got two words she can use.'

He pointed at the calendar on the wall. 'It's April, and we're in Australia,' he said loudly. 'AY-PRIL. ORS-TRAY-YAAAAH.'

In reply, the girl wrinkled her nose and frowned harder. Harley could tell from her expression that she thought he was making nonsense noises.

'Harley, love, she doesn't appear to be hard of hearing,' his mum said gently. 'She just doesn't understand any of *this*.' Delia flapped a hand at the room. 'I think she's got practically no frame of reference other than the words for *people* and *day*. I mean, look at her. She's not from *now*, is she? She's wearing some kind of full ceremonial costume and had something to do with that old vase that's in pieces in your bedroom, hard as it is to believe.'

'So?' Harley said, bewildered.

'So,' Delia's reply was patient, 'she needs our *help*.'

Delia, understanding a thing or two about people

in extreme distress, knew she was right. 'We have to help her. Even if I *am* knackered, and none of us is eating anytime soon because someone forgot to turn the oven on.'

Harley's stomach chose that moment to rumble loudly, as if in reproach.

Delia stepped further into the sitting room and, warily, the girl stepped back, her hands flying up into a defensive position, as if anticipating trouble. Delia paused with her own hands up in the air in a gesture of peaceful surrender. Quietly and calmly, she told Harley to fetch her phone from her handbag in the hallway. 'I need you to look something up for me, darl.'

He backed away, spotting the handbag wedged beside the umbrella stand next to the door. As he felt around inside for his mum's phone, he could see the girl desperately paging through the old dictionary again, frustration etched all over her delicate features.

Still in the same calm low tone, Delia told Harley, 'Look up where in Melbourne you can find old Chinese textbooks – you know, history and language books. It's got to be *old*. Pre-twentieth century.'

Harley typed in a few search terms. 'Like this one?'

Delia looked over her shoulder at the images Harley had pulled up: photographic reproductions of the pages of some old book. He scrolled through dozens of photos – someone had painstakingly photographed every pair of facing pages – with the heading *Zhu, English through the Vernaculars of the Canton and Shiuhing Prefectures, c.1862.*

'It's like an old guidebook that's filled with English phrases, with loads of Chinese written around the bits in English. That's gotta be helpful, right? Maybe she can borrow it and learn how to say some stuff so that we can figure out what she wants.'

'I'm not sure that phrasebook's quite old enough, actually,' Delia murmured, squinting at the photographs of the rough-looking sewn-together volume with Chinese and English words wood-blocked onto the pages. 'That tunic she has on looks, ah, pre-nineteenth century if my knowledge of kung fu soap operas is anything to go by.' She shook her head in disbelief at the words coming out of her mouth. 'Where's the book?'

'At the State Library,' Harley said, scrolling

through more pages of the book before zooming in on a section headed by the phrase *Can you help me?* in a flowing cursive script with Chinese characters around it. 'The library has tonnes of other Chinese and English phrasebooks, maps and images of Chinese people from the nineteenth century, and even before that. But it's closed now, Mum, isn't it?'

Harley handed the phone to his mum, who in turn held it out to the girl, indicating frantically that she not take it, only look at it. Under the girl's nose, Delia navigated to the photographed page with *Can you help me?* written on it, before zooming back out and showing the girl the other photographed pages of the old book. The girl's eyes seemed to light up, or more accurately, glow with excitement.

And the whites of her eyes really *were* the faintest bit gold, Harley thought to himself, astonished.

The girl did the stamping thing with her foot again, then jabbed at the screen before turning her hand palm up.

'I think she's asking *Where?*' Harley murmured, standing at a safe distance behind his mum as the girl stamped her foot once more and made the same gesture with her hand.

Delia showed the girl a picture of the State Library – a grand, classical Victorian building of stone with a central peaked portico supported by eight massive carved pillars, huge wings running either side, a sweeping set of stairs leading up to the vast front entrance and a great domed reading room that rose from the centre of it all, at least five storeys high. 'It's a public library, love,' Delia added in what she hoped was a helpful tone. 'I can take you there tomorrow, first thing, to look at the book. I'm on late shift. But Harley's right, it's probably closed now.'

The word floated up out of Delia's memory from a murky, long ago somewhere. '*Guān*,' she said in Chinese. 'You know, closed.'

The girl cocked her head and opened her mouth as if she wanted to say something at last, but she shut it again, dropping the heavy dictionary. It fell to the ground with a thud. The girl made a rapid writing motion with her hand instead.

'She wants to write something, Mum,' Harley said.

'I can see that,' his mum said, looking around the room for a piece of paper or a pen. 'But, as usual, there isn't a bit of stationery in the entire wretched place.'

Harley took the phone out of his mum's hand and turned it to the landscape position.

He opened a drawing application before Delia could react, showing the girl how to draw on it with a finger by doing a smiley face. He erased the smiley face and the girl reached for the phone eagerly. But before she could take it from him, Harley pointed at the conspicuously dead TV behind her and waggled his free hand. 'Less power,' he said in a more normal speaking voice, hoping she understood the tone, if not the words. 'Don't make it die.'

'I need that phone, Harls,' his mum wailed under her breath as the girl took it from him without touching him this time, turning the phone over in her hand and feeling its weight before orienting it to landscape again and studying the screen. 'It's got my entire life in it, Harley – my shifts for the next three months, all your parent–teacher interviews, you shouldn't have…'

Delia fell silent. The girl had placed the index finger of her right hand against the right of the screen and was drawing in quick, contained strokes. When she held the image out to Harley and Delia they each got goosebumps.

The girl pointed at the silken creatures twining across her tunic, and Delia said, 'Okay, dragon. Got it.'

The girl hesitated for a moment before inscribing a simple character to the left of the dragon image.

Lastly, she drew one box inside another beside that:

Then the girl handed the phone back to Harley with exaggerated care, not touching his hand.

'Read it from right to left,' Delia said. 'I don't remember much, but I do remember that.'

Harley sat down on the edge of the couch and

flicked out of the drawing application, plugging a round of new search terms into his mum's phone as he compared lists of common Chinese characters against the simple hand-drawn characters that had followed the symbol of the dragon.

When he glanced up at his mother at last, Harley looked shaky.

'What?' Delia said. 'What does it say? Is it a name? A place?'

Harley shook his head, flicking back to the screen of words and images the girl had drawn. He gave a little shiver as he peered down at them.

'It's a message. She's written: *Dragon. King. Returns.*'

Chapter 3

Delia's blood ran cold, but before she could pepper
Harley with questions – questions that she knew
he wouldn't have answers to – the girl slipped right
past them, out of the room. They turned to stare
at each other, shocked, before following the fleeing
figure back down the hallway to Harley's bedroom,
watching as she bent and sifted through the pieces
of broken pottery on the floor as if she were looking
for something specific.

She was. Holding the thicker jagged base piece
up to the light, the girl turned it over and cried out –
the first sound the Sparks had heard her make.

On the base, Harley and his mum saw a small

red square with some white Chinese script on it like a potter's mark. Beneath the mark, like an afterthought, ran three horizontal lines that grew bigger as they went down, executed by hand in the same red glaze.

☰

'That's the character for *three*,' Delia breathed. 'I'm sure of it.'

'Wish I could get a closer look at that other mark,' Harley whispered back.

The girl closed her hand around the broken base of the vase – which was only slightly smaller than her palm – and bowed her head over it, as if in grief. It was as though she'd forgotten that Harley and his mum were standing there.

When she looked up again, Delia and Harley both gasped in shock. The irises of the girl's eyes were almost completely black now, the thin ring of azure swallowed almost to the edges by a hue like midnight, the whites glowing a darker gold.

The girl began to chant: short, sharp syllables, slippery as beads strung together without pause, that Harley couldn't catch and keep in his brain.

The room grew colder and colder as the chanting increased in volume and the Sparks' exhalations began to stain the air in little puffs of arctic white.

Without warning, the girl opened her hands at waist level, pushing them outwards with great force as she roared a word that sounded like *long*. At that moment, all the lights went out in the house, and through his bedroom window Harley saw the world outside go dark too.

It seemed like just a few seconds later that the lights came back on, but the girl was gone, and a heavy rain had begun to fall.

Instinct made Harley sprint down the hall and throw open the front door. He scanned the night sky outside and caught it – just a flash of azure blue through the leaves of the plane trees that lined his street on either side. Like blue lightning, but climbing *upwards*.

Harley scrambled for the bike and helmet he kept on the front veranda for emergencies just like this one.

'Where are you going, Harls?' his mum yelled behind him. 'It's pouring!'

'The State Library!' Harley shouted before he jammed his helmet on his head, kicked the brakes off, and rode straight down the front steps through the open gate and out into the street.

'You know I'll be all right, Mum!' Harley yelled back as his mother shrieked, '*Haar*-leeey *Spaaark*!'

Delia had a loud voice – just about everybody they knew agreed on that – and it followed Harley down the road like a banshee until he turned the corner into High Street and started pumping his legs furiously in the direction of the city, where the library was. His mum would stop being mad at him soon, he figured, because she trusted him to do the right thing. She always said so.

Harley couldn't be absolutely sure that the State Library was where the girl was headed, but when a sizzle of lightning lit up the sky for miles around, he knew he was right as he spotted a streak of brilliant blue high up, like a faint, sinuous ribbon of colour, heading across town. Harley turned in the same direction, the lightning followed by a boom of thunder so loud he almost fell off his bicycle as he ducked into a side street. But he rode on, grimly, through puddles of water on the road and dirty great waves which passing cars splashed up into his face. He cut through the green leafy parkland around the Shrine and the Domain before hitting the edge of the city and pedalling straight up Swanston Street, zipping and weaving through a clog of trams and crisscrossing pedestrians.

Outside the State Library, Harley leant his bike up against the base of the giant bronze statue of Joan of Arc on a horse. The building's façade was illuminated with golden spotlights, but Harley didn't spy any activity around the place other than a security guard checking that the front doors were locked. The guard's eyes moved disinterestedly over Harley standing in the rain before the man disappeared out of view into the gloom of the vast public library.

The rain stopped as suddenly as it had begun. Harley waited and waited in Joan of Arc's shadow, unsure what he was expecting to see, but expecting something. If you didn't count the police team trying to take down his dad that time when he was five, this was the most exciting thing that had ever happened in his life.

It was a weeknight, and the passing trams and people had thinned out. Harley finally drifted away from Saint Joan and onto the footpath below the front stairs. From where he was standing at street level, at an angle to the brilliantly lit portico with its triangular roof and soaring columns, he could see the central dome of the reading room quite clearly above the rest of the building. The heart of the building was dark.

Maybe he'd been wrong about where the girl was headed. Maybe she was just… gone.

If he'd been her and somehow got stuck inside a manky old vase, he'd have wanted to make himself scarce the first chance he got, too.

Dispirited and completely sodden, Harley began walking back towards Saint Joan to retrieve his bike – and froze as he spotted a tiny but bright glow in one of the three small uppermost windows of the East Wing. One moment the windows had been dark and, the next, there it was. Just a faint, will-o'-the-wisp gleam moving from window to window before winking out.

Barely breathing, Harley moved backwards to where he could see the tops of both wings and the dome. And about five seconds later, he saw the same faint darting light in the three darkened uppermost windows of the West Wing.

It could be the security guard moving his torch about, Harley thought. But how could the security guard have gotten there so quickly? He couldn't have run from the East Wing to the West Wing that fast even if he were an Olympic gold medallist on jet-powered rollerblades. Harley knew from a past school excursion that the building was absolutely enormous, with kilometres of passageways.

When, mere seconds later, the light started moving again against the glass-paned, octagonal dome of the vast reading room at the heart of the State Library – a dome at least five storeys high based on the number of the windows on the outside – Harley felt a thrill. He stood there, open-mouthed, as the light came and went, appearing at many of the multi-storeyed windows in the reading room edifice. Harley listened intently from where he was positioned outside the building, but no alarms were going off. There was just that tiny glow flitting from floor to floor, side to side, up and down, as if the laws of physics were a minor inconvenience to be disregarded.

She was looking for something.

Hours later, when the brilliant façade of the library and all the surrounding city buildings – the university, the train station, the big shopping complex – suddenly plunged into a moment of darkness so inky black it might have been the end of the world, right then and there, Harley just smiled.

When the lights of the buildings flashed back on within seconds, followed by sheet lightning so brilliant, and a crack of thunder so loud, that two passing students jumped and screamed, Harley climbed back on his bike and began retracing his journey.

He was still smiling when the rain came pelting down hard enough, it felt like, to take his skin off.

Delia had the front door open before he could even walk his bike back up the steps of the house. Before his mum had a chance to utter a word, Harley reminded her, 'Great-grandpa *did* always say there were things of great mystery and power in the world.'

Delia nodded, quoting softly, *'Just because you never see them, doesn't mean they're not there.'*

Because Delia did remember the stories her family used to tell about ghosts and spirits and old gods, and because she'd pretty much seen everything and hardly ever lost her cool, her extreme relief at Harley's safe return just before midnight manifested itself in the form of a gruff admonition. 'She's asleep on the couch in the dining room; got in just before you. Don't you dare wake her. She looked exhausted.'

When Harley passed the dining room-slash-study on the way to a hot shower that he needed right down to his bones, he could only see the dim shape of the girl curled up under a spare blanket with her face turned to the back of the couch. She looked so small and defenceless it was hard to believe the busted old vase, the melted TV and the spooky night-time trip to the library had really happened.

With a gluey chunk of twice-reheated pasta bake in his belly, Harley had slept like a log. But he was woken by the sound of his mum in the kitchen, turning up the radio for the hourly news bulletin. Warm, drowsy and confused, Harley didn't immediately know what day it was, or make any move to spring out of bed, until he heard what the newsreader was saying.

And in breaking local news, the State Library has reported a puzzling break-in overnight that saw books primarily from the Linguistics, Australiana and China collections scattered throughout the galleries of the famed domed Reading Room. Thousands of volumes were taken off their shelves and left open by what is thought to have been a gang of well-read intruders, without security becoming aware of the activities until the early hours of the morning. A massive clean-up operation is underway. Nothing appears to have been taken, although security measures are under urgent review.

Harley stumbled through the kitchen door in his blue flannel alien pyjamas, with his black hair sticking up all one side of his head and pillow creases across his face. He recoiled when he saw the girl sitting at the table. Her intricately embroidered tunic, skirt and slippers were immaculate – showing no signs of having been slept in – and her hair fell in sleek wings across her collarbones. She studied Harley with an unfathomable expression over the rim of her glass before taking a sip.

Which reminded Harley of how thirsty he was. With a tongue like sandpaper, he croaked, 'Water, please,' as he sat down across the table from the girl.

'That's exactly what *she's* been asking for,' Delia said thoughtfully, filling a matching tall glass from the tap and handing it to her son before moving across to the toaster. 'She hasn't wanted anything *but* water.'

'She's been *asking*?' Harley exclaimed, glass halfway to his lips.

'We've been having a lovely chat,' Delia said. 'Haven't we, pet?'

The girl actually nodded, and Harley choked.

'She's one of five,' Delia continued, pushing a plate of toast across the table towards Harley. 'You're hard enough work for anyone. I never would have been able to cope with *five*.'

'You're making that up, Mum,' Harley said through the toast in his mouth.

'Show him,' Delia told the girl, a touch smugly. 'The way you showed me.'

Looking at Delia, the girl said, '*Mā ma* Delia,' and held up her index finger to indicate the number one; she then used that same finger to point at Harley.

'Mama Delia has one child.' Delia beamed. 'That's right. I understood her straight away.'

Harley coughed a bit of chewed-up toast onto

the table, and the girl wrinkled her nose in disgust. 'She can talk now?'

'No *mā ma*,' the girl continued, pointing at herself. 'Only *bà ba*.'

'That's the Chinese word for father,' Delia said helpfully. 'She's saying she's got a dad, which is nice.'

The girl repeated, '*Bà ba*,' before holding up five fingers then producing the shard of pottery from somewhere in her voluminous clothing. She pushed it across the table towards Harley, tapping at the symbol for three inked on it.

Then she pointed at herself.

'Maybe she's saying she's three years old,' Harley snorted. 'I mean, it's not like she can say much. She might as well be three.'

'*Harley*,' Delia admonished.

The girl gave Harley a dark look before retrieving something else from her tunic so quickly that Harley didn't actually see her hands move.

She slid a piece of tattered paper across the table towards him and his mum.

They gasped.

'Is that what I *think* it is?' Delia said to the girl reproachfully over Harley's head. 'You can't go around doing that to *books*. Especially not old library books that are supposed to be for everyone.'

'I'm not even allowed to dog-ear any pages,' Harley said, his eyes wide.

Somehow, in that vast dark library filled with millions of books, the girl had located the nineteenth-century Chinese–English phrasebook that they'd shown her on Delia's phone the night before.

The Sparks stared down in astonishment at the very page – printed on brittle, falling-apart paper – that had *Can you help me?* wood-blocked across the top in a combination of spidery English script and neat but complicated-looking Chinese characters.

The girl gently placed the broken piece from the vase on top of the paper and looked from mother to son with liquid eyes.

Delia's expression softened. 'I know it's an emergency, but just don't do that again to another book for as long as you live,' she admonished. 'And we will. We *will* help you.'

Amazingly, the girl nodded as if she understood.

'Now you know that I'm *Delia*,' Delia continued, placing her hands on Harley's shoulders from behind. 'And this shoddy-looking individual is called *Harley*.'

The girl looked at Harley gravely, then placed a hand on her chest and said, '*Qing*,' in a low voice with a strange, but pleasant, resonance.

Then she tapped the red potter's mark on the pottery shard.

'You want us to help you find out who...*made* this?' Harley frowned. 'How would we do that? It's heaps old. I wouldn't know where to begin.'

Harley felt his mum's hands go rigid on his shoulders, her fingers like claws, as if she'd suddenly thought of something quite dreadful.

'Ow,' he said, twisting his head around to look at his mum. 'You're hurting me!'

'How old do you think that is?' Delia whispered, staring straight ahead, as though gripped by an idea. 'Do you think it's...valuable?'

Harley snorted, and the girl watched them both intently over the glass of water she was draining. She held the glass out for more, and Delia turned like a zombie towards the sink with the glass as Harley said, '*Was* valuable, you mean. It's in pieces in my wastepaper bin, remember?'

His mother handed the glass back to the girl, who drank thirstily from it again. 'Anyway, it was on the footpath outside Hammonds the Auctioneers,' Harley went on, feeling a stab of shame. 'It didn't look valuable. Someone had just left it there like they'd forgotten it.'

'Harley Spark!' Delia rounded on her son. 'Don't tell me you just helped yourself to that vase?'

'It looked like it had just come out of a hole in the ground,' Harley mumbled sheepishly. 'Honestly! And where would we even begin to look for the person who made that – given that you know fewer than thirty of the three hundred most common Chinese words, Mum, let alone the, uh, *fifty thousand* others?'

His mother's glazed eyes snapped back to the girl, who had placed her empty glass down between them on the table like a challenge.

Delia squeezed her eyes shut for a second at the

thought of her ex-husband. 'We begin with your father, Harley,' she snapped. 'Go get your special telephone. Hurry.'

Chapter 4

When Ray Spark had given Harley the special telephone for his thirteenth birthday in the back room of one of Ray's favourite pizza restaurants, he had instructed Harley, 'This is only to be used for emergencies. If you can't reach me on my normal number, I'll always be reachable on this one.' Ray had pointed to a special DAD icon on the screen which Harley didn't really take in at the time because he was too busy stuffing his face with pizza. Compared to his fossil collection, Harley found phones kind of *meh* and usually forgot to carry his, charge it or even turn it on. What did he need another phone for?

Ray had squeezed Harley's face between his hands so that Harley was forced to stop chewing for a moment to look at him. 'No matter where I am in the world, you can get me on this phone. But you can't just ring me on it to tell me what the football score is. There's satellite technology involved here, and a network of at least a million favours. It's got to be life and death, okay?'

Harley had laughed. 'Like if I'm chained by my wrists above a shark pool? I can use it then?'

And Ray had smiled his charming, easy, eye-crinkling smile that made a dimple appear in his right cheek in the same place it did on Harley's face when *he* smiled, and agreed, 'The exact situation.'

Harley said to his mum now, 'This isn't *life and death*, Mum.'

'For her it might be,' Delia growled. 'Get the phone. I want to see whether it does what Ray says it does. I could never even reach him to tell him the gas company was coming to turn off the gas – all those times they came to turn off the gas – because he'd forgotten to pay a bill and was "out of the country". I want to know whether he's making things up, as usual.'

Harley went back into his bedroom and opened the middle drawer of his desk where he kept Ray's special phone in an old biscuit tin. Harley hadn't turned it on since he'd charged it almost two weeks ago because no actual *life and death* situations had eventuated. Maybe it was flat. Harley hoped it was. His dad might have been using a jokey tone of voice when he'd explained why the *special telephone* was special, but he hadn't actually been joking. Harley knew him well enough to know when he was being deadly serious. This phone was not to be used lightly.

Harley walked back into the kitchen with it and said uncertainly, 'Can't we just try him on your phone first on his usual number?'

To which Delia snapped, 'And get one of his giant goons like Ivan or Schumacher on the line and have to talk about the weather in Krakow or Bavaria when they last visited their mums? I don't think so. Give me that.' She held her hand out impatiently as Qing looked, wide-eyed, from mother to son, the faintest hint of amusement in her expression.

'But it's *my* special telephone,' Harley whined.

Delia gave Harley a speaking look and swiped it out of his hand. She turned it over a few times, weighing it in her palm, much as Qing had done with Delia's own phone the night before.

It was small and flat and silver and, from the back, looked like a polished business-card case from the 1920s. From the front, it looked like a normal phone except that it had no home button. It had no visible means of being switched on.

Delia looked across the table at Qing, who sat back slightly in her chair and crossed her arms, her bell-like sleeves at odds with her businesslike posture. 'Ray bought me an air conditioner one birthday that turned out to have nothing inside it except sawdust,' Delia said, shaking her head. 'This could be from the same batch of *special* things.'

She handed the small silver phone back to her son, rolling her eyes. 'It's pretty, but there's no way of turning it on. Good one, Ray.'

Harley shook his head. 'Yes there is, Mum. It's "special" because of this.'

He placed the phone in his left palm and pressed his right thumb into the centre of the screen, holding it there for exactly three seconds: *one-cat-and-dog*, *two-cat-and-dog*, *three-cat-and-dog* – the way Ray had told him to.

The phone lit up with the faintest *whirr* and *click*,

vibrating gently in Harley's hand to say that it was awake and ready.

A bright-red symbol appeared where his thumb had been. Delia and Qing bent closer to look at it.

'Biometrics, Mum.' It was Harley's turn to sound smug. 'It only turns on for *me*, Dad said. He had it made that way.'

Qing made a small noise that might have been a whistle, the whites of her eyes glowing just a little more gold than before.

The red symbol dissolved and the three of them bent their heads over the screen, which now had dozens of icons on it. Harley thought a lot of them had to represent maps – the icons had names under them like *Venice*, *Jakarta*, *Mogadishu*, and one he had no hope of pronouncing: *Llanfairpwllgwyngyll*.

Harley pointed at the bright red icon simply labelled with **DAD**. 'As in *red* for a situation of *imminent danger*,' he said dryly, looking around the Sparks' shabby kitchen. 'Just like this one.'

'Don't be smart,' Delia retorted. 'Does it take photos?'

Harley nodded, easily finding the camera icon.

Delia pushed the shard of pottery towards the edge of the kitchen table, and Harley zoomed in on it and took a good clear shot in the bright sunlight flooding in through the kitchen window. The potter's mark and numeral three were easy to see because, just like Ray's own logo, they were the bright red of fresh blood.

'Send it to him,' Delia said. 'I want to see what happens; whether he gets back to us in three hours, or three years.'

Harley tucked the tip of his tongue into the corner of his mouth – which was what he did when he was really concentrating – pressed the *Share* icon and wrote:

> **Dad, we need to find out who made this
> or where it came from, URGENTLY
> (Mum says this qualifies as life and death,
> it was not my call). H**

Then he sent the snap and message to *Dad*, the only contact in the contact list besides *Mum*, and placed the silver phone gently on the table.

'Send *me* a message,' Delia muttered. 'I want to be able to reach you on your "special" phone.'

Harley hastily complied, then everyone waited with their breath held until they started seeing spots, but nothing happened.

'Right,' Delia said in the tone of deep and customary disappointment she reserved for her former husband. 'Who's for pancakes then?'

She stalked away from the table and crouched to rummage through the pots and pans drawer below the kitchen counter for the frying pan. Harley stared at Qing and Qing stared at Harley as if they were in Mexico and this was a stand-off.

No one expected the little silver phone to give a sharp double *ping*, least of all Delia, who jumped so high that she clipped her head on the edge of the counter and fell backwards onto the floor at Harley's feet with the frying pan in her hands.

Shivering violently as if it were cold, the little phone kept double-*pinging* until Harley stuck his thumb back into the centre of the screen and they all read what was on it.

Call me now. Your mum's right. It COULD be life and death. For me.

Ray's first words were, 'I know a bloke.'

He didn't even say *Hello, Harls*; that was how serious it was.

'I sent the pic to two fellas I know, Harley, and this one bloke comes back to me not even a sparrow's fart later and says, *Bring me the piece in question and any other pieces you've got.* So I say, *My boy's got the piece in question*, and he says, *Has he told anyone else about it?* And I say, *Noooo* (forgetting to tell him about the other bloke because I can't get a word in edgeways and, anyway, they hate each other's guts), and *he* says, *Good, it's worth a bleeding fortune if it's legit, because it's part of one of the rarest pieces in the Pan-Asiatic antiquities market. Everybody who's anybody is after this potter's work. Even. Rarer. Than. Hen's. Teeth. GET YOUR BOY TO TROT IT IN QUICK SMART*, he shouts. And *bang*, the phone goes dead.'

There was the forlorn, muffled honking sound of a sea bird in the background. 'Where are you exactly, Dad?' Harley exclaimed, impressed, despite himself, at the abilities and excellent sound quality of the little silver phone.

And Ray said hastily, 'On a parapet in Budapest – well, technically in Buda, not Pest – at a little, uh … travel expo some blokes have organised here.'

Delia – whose cheek was squished up against Harley's to hear better – mouthed: *A likely story.*

'Tell your mum (I know she's listening) that…'

Harley went cold with horror at the thought that his dad was about to say something Harley couldn't ever un-hear, like, *Tell your mum I love her and have always loved her.*

He glanced sideways at his mum and saw that her eyes had gone all shiny and her face had gone red the way it always did when she thought about Ray Spark and *the things that might have been.*

All the way over in Budapest, Ray cleared his throat. 'Tell your mother,' he said, his voice suddenly furtive and low as if he had company, 'seeing as how it's life and death for me, being in the, ah, business that I'm in, to drive you to ANTEDILUVIAN HOUSE. Got that? Antediluvian House. Right this minute. To see that bloke. He knows his stuff. Garstang J. Runyon runs an antiquities, uh…' there was that moment of hesitation again, '…valuations and restoration business. It's the southern hemisphere's epicentre of Pan-Asiatic antiquities knowledge. No one knows more about broken bits of Chinese pottery than that bloke. He was *salivating* to see it. He kept saying, *The seal! The seal!* And I don't think he meant saltwater-dwelling mammals. You want to help your old man, don't you, Harley? Doing this safe, simple, tiny thing for me will unlock a thousand favours.'

The lone sea bird honked again, this time so close to Ray's mouthpiece that Harley could have sworn he was on the phone to an albatross rather than his dad. 'Gotta go, Harls,' Ray murmured hastily. 'The travel expo is hotting up.' Then the line went dead.

There was a loud clatter – the sound a pine dining chair makes as it falls backwards onto a slate-tiled floor. Delia and Harley looked away from the phone, startled, as Qing rose to her feet. Her eyes were going black again – the dark centres edging out the ring of bright blue – and the room was already turning arctic as Delia reached across the table without hesitation. Now was not the time.

She latched grimly onto Qing's narrow shoulders – though the static shocks were awful and continuous, like sticking her fingers into a power point – and shook the girl gently. 'No flying off in broad daylight, love – not unless you want to be taken out by a weather reporter or a police chopper. *If,* I decide to indulge Ray and his "simple favour"', Delia snorted, 'we'd take the car. I'd find this Antediluvian House much faster than you can because a nice lady lives inside my car's satnav who can direct us there, all right?'

Qing blinked twice, rapidly; the ring of blue returned to her dark irises and the air began to edge back from what felt like absolute zero towards maybe two degrees Celsius. She seemed to give herself a mental shake; then she smiled, which broke up the usually serious contours of her angular face in new and charming ways.

It was the first time she had smiled since the vase broke.

🜨

Harley followed Delia around the kitchen on his knees, resolutely begging, until his mum finally agreed that the first two periods of school were out of the question at a *life and death* time like this one. A little detour through Chinatown was in order.

Harley, Delia and Qing crossed the backyard to Delia's ancient hatchback not ten minutes later, Delia clutching the plastic bag containing all of the broken pieces of the vase apart from the base. Qing flatly refused to give up that bit.

Harley nudged his mum as she pulled out her car keys. 'What's an *Antediluvian* House as opposed to any other kind?'

Delia didn't answer until she'd gently ushered Qing into the back seat and clipped her in, getting another bad static shock for her troubles and earning an apologetic shrug from the girl that seemed to say, *My bad, I cause these all the time. I can't help it.*

Staring over the roof of the car at Harley, who was about to climb into the front seat, Delia replied, 'Antediluvian means *before the Flood.*'

Puzzled, Harley said, 'Which flood?'

Delia's mouth assumed the poker-straight line it always did when Harley asked her a question she wasn't keen on answering. She got in behind the wheel and pressed the remote on the rear gate that led out into the laneway behind the house as Harley, who was now strapped in beside her, persisted. 'Come on, Mum. What could possibly be so special about the things inside Antediluvian House and Dad's "bloke"? He knows heaps of blokes. None of the ones we know of are remotely special. Which flood?'

Delia backed out into the crooked bluestone lane running down the rear of their house. Still without responding, she woke the nice lady who lived inside her car's satnav, typing the words *Antediluvian House* into the little screen sitting on top of the faded dashboard.

'*Antediluvian House*,' the virtual lady enunciated brightly, and the girl in the back seat sat bolt upright, all her attention fixed on the front of the car in wonder. Delia watched in the driver's mirror as Qing looked all around the car's interior, trying to work out where the sound was coming from and how it was being done.

'*Continue north along Oxley Street for 687 metres...*'

'Mum,' Harley shouted over the nice lady droning on about *left turns*, *right turns* and *northbound on-ramps*. 'Which flood?!'

Distracted by the flow of directions, Delia replied faintly, 'The one in the Bible. Even though it's a gigantic case of false advertising, you can assume that everything inside Antediluvian House is absolutely *ancient*.'

Harley shot his mum a shocked look as she added, 'Like the vase *she* came out of.'

The Sparks both glanced at Qing, feeling a chill as they realised the girl was staring straight back at them with a frown faintly pleating her brow as if she'd understood every word they'd just said.

Chapter 5

Antediluvian House turned out to be a three-storey Victorian red-brick building with white painted trim, jammed between two dumpling restaurants in Chinatown. There were three narrow windows on the ground floor and four windows on each of the upper floors. The double front doors at street level – with the number 116A painted on one of them in a tidy hand – appeared to be made of solid steel and were firmly locked. The glass panes in every single window were completely covered in white paint so that no one could see in, or out. Harley had probably walked past the building hundreds of times in his life, but had never even noticed it was there.

He banged on the doors with the flat of his hand and looked across the road at his mum, who'd parked in a construction loading zone and was hoping for the best.

He mouthed to her, 'What do I do?' when there was no answer from within the building.

There was no visible way of getting the attention of whoever was inside. There wasn't a doorbell, security camera or peephole to be seen. The doors didn't even have handles on the outside. Their dull red paint was worn, as if many visitors had placed their desperate hands on them, in just the same way Harley was doing now. In order to keep his hands free for doing things like banging on locked doors, Harley had shoved the plastic bag full of ceramic fragments into the front of his zipped-up tartan bomber jacket, and the pieces were digging into his flannel shirt front uncomfortably.

Beside him, Qing studied the doors from top to bottom, running her hands over the thin seam between the two giant steel panels. Scanning the largely empty street around them quickly, she placed her right hand flat against a point about her shoulder-height and closed her eyes. Her lips moved silently for a moment, though no sound came out.

Harley felt a distinct, sharp chill in the air.

Qing pushed on one of the doors and it swung slightly open. She slipped inside noiselessly without a backward glance.

Open-mouthed, Harley looked back at his mum, pointing furiously at the gap, and Delia's window slid down. 'Ray and his simple favours! If you're not out in fifteen minutes, I'm calling emergency services,' she yelled. 'If they don't arrive first, that is, and give me a big fat parking ticket.'

The hallway Harley found himself in as he swung the steel door shut behind him was dark and empty. He felt gingerly along the bare wooden floor with the toes of his sneakered feet, hissing, 'Qing? Qing?'

There was no sign of the girl. When his face got entangled in something soft hanging at the end of the hall, Harley bellowed in surprise, stumbling and flailing through the curtain into a big room that took up the entire ground floor.

He gasped; his nose was only inches away from a life-sized, finely detailed horse made of fired clay, pulling a polished wooden chariot. Looking up, he flinched at the looming figure of a moustachioed Chinese charioteer in long robes and full armour, hair in a neat topknot beneath a kind of fan-shaped crown, one fist raised as if to strike Harley down.

Arranged behind the charioteer, all across the big room, were dozens more soldiers, all life-sized, with different facial expressions and military uniforms – most with armour, some without – hair bound up in neat topknots or wearing crowns or hats or hoods. There were rows of them – all made of fired clay. It was the eeriest, most awe-inspiring thing Harley had ever seen.

He walked along the front row of standing infantrymen gingerly, so close that he could see tiny flakes of ancient paint still stuck to their faces, hands, clothes and toe-capped shoes. All along the walls, giant tapestries and ink paintings depicted fierce battles, soldiers in chariots and sheaves of flying arrows; men everywhere on horseback, and on foot. On the back wall of the huge room, two steel brackets held up a lethal-looking black sword with a ridged blade and an unusual, elongated hilt capable of a two-handed grip, the whole weapon almost as long as Harley was tall.

Someone had clearly taken a lot of care with the display; the whole room was lit by soft and modern downlighting, and there wasn't a speck of dust to be seen on any surface. The disreputable exterior of Antediluvian House didn't even hint at the wonders inside.

A soft, very serpentine *hiss* emanated from a dim corner at the back of the vast room and Harley squinted to see Qing pointing upwards. She placed her foot on the first stair of a narrow wooden staircase and flitted up out of sight. Sucking in his gut so that it wouldn't accidently brush against any of the warrior statues and send them crashing down like dominoes, Harley wove across the room in her wake, the broken vase pieces jiggling uncomfortably against him.

Unlike Qing, whose progress upwards was silent and undetectable, Harley set off a different creak in every stair along the way, which meant that when he reached the light-flooded first floor – which had an internal glass skylight set into its ceiling and was filled with priceless pottery, bronze and stone figurines, ornaments and implements in gleaming, lit-up display cases – he found himself face to face with a short, elderly man with at least three chins, and no hair or eyebrows. The man was shaped kind of like a lopsided Humpty Dumpty, but there was no time to feel even mildly amused because he was levelling a black handgun right at Harley's sternum.

'Who *are* you?' the hairless man barked in an American accent, his head suspended like a huge, misshapen bowling ball above a black turtleneck jumper and voluminous beige cargo trousers, their lumpy pockets jammed with tools and brushes. 'How did you get in?'

The old man had colourless eyes and bad teeth and was the scariest-looking individual Harley had ever seen.

'I'm Ray Spark's boy, Harley? The door was open? I brought that broken vase? For you to look at, sir, so don't shoot me?' Harley was so nervous everything was coming out as a high, squeaky question.

The man lowered his handgun a little so that it was now aimed in a slightly friendlier fashion at Harley's bellybutton instead of at the centre of his chest.

'Perhaps I did leave it open, I'm a little forgetful when I'm working,' the man muttered through thin, colourless lips. 'Garstang J. Runyon,' he barked by way of introduction. 'Ray's boy, eh? I was expecting one of Ray's usual boys.' The old man's smile was humourless. 'One of his six-foot-seven ones in head-to-toe black leather with matching brass knuckledusters and brass toe caps on their military-issue boots. Where's the seal then? Quickly, lad.'

Harley patted his front hastily to indicate he was taking something out and Garstang waved at him to do it, although Harley noted he wasn't putting his gun away. Harley held the plastic bag full of ceramic fragments out to the antiquities expert, who snatched it away quickly, peering inside and grunting, 'It looks like a particularly fine Ru Ware glaze, nearly white. But the seal's not here.' The old man sifted in vain through the bag for the telltale red markings that had been in the intriguing image Ray Spark had sent him.

'*She's* got it.' Harley's eyes flickered past the armed man in the direction of a ceiling-high painted statue of a god in a Chinese helmet and colourful robes of red and gold and blue. A long, wiry black beard and moustache flowed down his chest, and he held a spear with a curved blade in one hand and a golden sword in the other.

For a man with terrible posture, so many chins and so few teeth, Garstang J. Runyon swung around pretty niftily on his feet. He gasped as Qing drifted out from behind the giant statue, the piece of pottery with the seal on it grasped in one of her small hands.

At the sight of the girl, the old man actually placed his gun down on top of the nearest glass display case, bowed in a formal-looking way and addressed Qing in Chinese. Qing smiled and inclined her head, but didn't respond any further. Garstang J. Runyon turned to Harley, his colourless eyes shining with emotion. 'I never thought I'd live to see the day,' he said. 'She's wearing full ceremonial court dress from the Warring States period featuring *six* imperial dragons with hand-carved, C-shaped Hongshan dragons in lapis lazuli on the belt ties. I've only ever seen paintings with anything near as fine in them.'

All Harley could reply in confusion was, 'I *knew* it was lapis lazuli,' as the old man widened his arms expansively and chuckled, 'This way, children, this way. Honoured, charmed and caught completely off guard – and *that* doesn't happen every day.'

The old man led Qing and Harley up the stairs to the top floor of the building, quite forgetting to pick up his black handgun as they made their way out of the room of priceless treasures.

On the uppermost level, the natural light was dazzling, courtesy of an even bigger skylight in the ceiling that illuminated what was clearly the old man's workspace. The brilliant sunlight cascaded down through the secondary skylight in the floor to the level below. It was an ingenious way to illuminate an otherwise dark Victorian-era warehouse.

Standing lamps with heads that could swivel or extend were positioned across the room. Around the rectangular secondary skylight set into the floor were arranged long wooden tables with antique artefacts balanced on stands, all in a state of disrepair. Old scrolls, books and papers lay scattered about, some open to particular images, or passages in flowing Chinese script. Across the room, against the back wall, stood the three-metre-tall statue of a beautiful goddess with a traditional, looping Chinese-bun hairstyle in clothes like the ones Qing was wearing, entirely carved out of a pale, almost translucent, polished jade. She was so finely wrought that her clothes – which lifted and curled at the hems and at the sleeves – seemed to be rippling and ruffling in an unearthly breeze. Harley imagined he could feel it, moving through the room.

Another life-sized terracotta horse stood sentry to the left of the goddess, and Qing ran across to it, face crinkled in delight, running her free hand lightly over the horse's muzzle as if she recognised the beast that it represented. After a moment, she turned away from the horse statue almost reluctantly and placed the pottery piece with the potter's mark on an empty stretch of workbench right under the old man's nose.

She stepped back and looked at him expectantly.

Garstang J. Runyon gave a sigh as if he were sinking into a particularly deep and luxurious bubble bath. He drew on a pair of white gloves that lay on a table nearby, then gently removed all of the pieces of the broken vase from Harley's plastic bag, arranging them around the base piece Qing had just surrendered.

Harley blinked in astonishment at the roughly reconstructed vase, radiating out in an exploded two dimensions from the base piece. Apart from the piece with the red markings, the entire vessel – still covered in a very fine network of cracks – now appeared to be white on both sides with the merest faint tint of blue in the glaze. The vase might never have had a dragon painted on the outside of it at all.

The old man placed a jeweller's loupe into one of his eyes and bent low, his pudgy nose almost touching the surface of the shattered vase as he swept his gaze across it. 'As fine as polished bone,' Garstang murmured, running a gloved fingertip over the surface of one of the pieces. 'Not Ru Ware, as I initially thought, but something even finer. If this potter's mark is to be believed ...' Garstang took the magnifier out of his eye and made his way across the room, with an ungainly, rolling gait, to the far corner, searching for something on a table covered in old scrolls of different sizes, '... the maker only ever made *fourteen* vases. Eight of which he never painted and left blank – in that exact shade, like snow with a hint of blue ice at its heart.' The old man flicked his gloved fingers in the direction of the shattered vase. 'I'd thought the unpainted ones were all safely locked up in the National Palace Museum in Taiwan. The curator told me himself, many, many years ago when I was posing as a— Oh, never mind. Anyway, he said that the other *six* vases were each said to feature a unique dragon, each one painted in a different dominant colour.'

'This was the blue one,' Harley said quickly.

'But it's *blank*,' Garstang replied, looking across

at Harley in disbelief. 'The fired image should never change.'

Harley's voice was insistent. 'Before it broke, it had a bright blue dragon on it, I swear.'

Qing shook her head fiercely as if disagreeing with them both and said, '*Qīng*,' the exact same way she said her own name. To Harley's untrained ear it sounded like *Ching*.

'This was the legendary Qing Long vase?' Garstang gaped from across the room, the scroll he'd been searching for clutched in one white-gloved hand. 'The vase that featured the Azure Dragon?'

Harley blinked as Qing nodded as if she'd understood every word the old man had just uttered.

'*But how?*' Garstang exclaimed.

He stumped across the room, sweeping a host of stone ink chops, bamboo-handled paintbrushes and rolls of silky paper to one side of a table before laying the scroll he was holding down gently, as if it were a sleeping baby. He carefully unrolled the brittle, handpainted scroll to its full length, gesturing impatiently at Harley to weigh down the edges with two carved stone lion statuettes that happened to be resting on the next table.

The script of the scroll was in a running, fluid

calligraphy even more impossible for Harley to make out than the printed Chinese characters he was used to seeing on shopfronts. There were no pictures, but the scroll was edged in a particularly complex and beautiful handwoven red and gold silk embossed with a repeating pattern of rampant dragons.

Qing made a bird-like noise of excitement, running her eyes down each column of characters until she came to a section near the end of the scroll that made her suddenly cover her mouth in distress. Fat tears fell out of her eyes onto the edge of the table.

When she looked across at Harley and Garstang, her lashes were still damp, and her eyes were bleak, the blue ring around each iris more prominent than usual. She did that thing with her hands that Harley had come to understand as meaning *Where?*

'Do you know what it says?' Harley asked the old man, who nodded his ponderous, shiny head.

'This scroll tells the legend of the five dragon sisters of the Wudang Mountains, near modern Hubei,' Garstang recounted quietly, looking from girl to scroll with a deep frown. 'All were daughters of the First Dragon, who ruled that region of China with a firm and just hand. Their names were Zhu Long (Vermilion Dragon), Huang Long (Yellow Dragon), Qing Long (Azure Dragon), Bai Long (White Dragon) and Hei Long (Black Dragon).'

Qing nodded and nodded as Harley pulled a drum-shaped porcelain stool out from under one of the work tables and sat down cautiously. Qing stood straighter, letting the trailing cuffs of her magnificently embroidered sleeves fall over her clasped hands, assuming a listening attitude.

'The Second Dragon,' the old man continued, 'who had nine sons and considered himself greater in power and majesty even than his own brother, had all five of his nieces abducted and delivered to a crippled old magician – Tiān Àn Jìn – to be killed.' The old man tapped a series of three characters on the scroll, indicating with a flick of his pudgy fingers that they had something in common with the potter's mark.

'The old magician – whose mark this is reputed to be – was servant to one of the four Diamond Kings of Heaven; the very Diamond King that you saw on the floor below, Mo Li Qing. And though the old magician owed the Second Dragon a favour for once having saved his life, the magician was very fond of the five girls. Legend has it that he cast each girl into a plain pottery prison, rather than kill them outright.'

Harley and Garstang both looked at Qing, whose face was unreadable. 'She can't possibly be…' the old man's voice fell to a mere whisper, '…number three dragon daughter, can she? According to the scroll, the vases were made then dispersed across China by the magician himself – in a series of arduous personal journeys – to keep the girls safe. Even if a word of it were true, boy, it would have happened almost two and a half thousand years ago.'

Stunned, Harley darted a glance at Qing, whose eyes were now screwed shut as if she were deep in thought. 'Say it *was* possible to, um, survive imprisonment inside a, ah, vase for that long,' Harley said, 'would it mean that there's a chance that the other sisters may also have survived? And why are there *five* other vases? Not four? You said there were six dragon vases. But there were only five sisters. I don't understand.'

Garstang shrugged, fumbling for his own

porcelain Chinese stool and sitting down heavily, his rear end overflowing the drum-shaped seat all around. 'The scroll is a creation myth, Harley. It can't be real. Whoever heard of a *Diamond King*? Or magicians with real powers like these? Dragons?'

Qing's eyes flashed open and she said fiercely, '*Real*. Where?' She jabbed her finger at the pieces of her own vase then spread her hand wide: five fingers to indicate five sisters.

She made that *Where?* gesture again as she pointed at the potter's mark, and the old man shook his head. 'If he ever was a real person, child, he would be dead. It's been too long.'

'No!' Qing hissed.

The old man replied gently, 'Apart from the eight blank vases, child, I know of only one other dragon vase in existence today. It's the centrepiece of a magnificent private collection in Singapore, owned by a very wealthy family that made its fortune in importation. Before the vase entered their collection, it was offered to me almost twenty years ago now, by the very person who—'

There was a resounding crash from the floor below, as if someone had just blundered face first into a giant terracotta warhorse and brought the whole beast tumbling down.

Garstang surged to his feet, searching in vain for his handgun. '*NO!*' he cried, waddling for the staircase.

Chapter 6

Qing and Harley exchanged glances, the girl's hands moving so quickly that Harley couldn't catch where she'd tucked away the piece of vase bearing the magician's mark inside her voluminous clothing.

They ran for the staircase leading down to the lower floors, but were stopped by Garstang J. Runyon's ample buttocks re-entering the room backwards, followed swiftly by the rest of him. 'The roof,' he said in a strangled voice over his shoulder. 'It's the only place to hide. Five of Chiu Chiu Pang's strongest bodyguards are coming up the stairs. I caught a glimpse of them through the glass skylight below. I don't know how they found out it was here, but they must want the vase – even in pieces it's worth more than half the buildings in Chinatown! You will understand, children, when I say *trust in Guan Yin to save you. It is the only way.* I beg you, *go.*'

Qing's eyes flashed to the giant jade Goddess of Mercy standing before the wall on the far side of the huge workroom, and she nodded quickly.

Harley and Qing backtracked towards the tall jade statue, avoiding stepping on the clear skylight in the floor so that their progress would not be seen from below. But they froze in their tracks as a woman's bloodcurdling shriek cut through the air, accompanied by sounds of violent struggle and breaking pottery.

'Run, Harley, run!' they heard Delia yell from two floors down.

Across the room, at the head of the staircase, Garstang made a strange grunting noise and crashed to the ground on his back. 'Run!' he gargled, echoing Delia's warning.

Harley, looking over his shoulder as he fled, felt his skin almost leap off his body as a man dressed in head-to-toe black with a balaclava over his face and wielding a thick length of bamboo pole as long as a man's forearm, stepped over Garstang's sprawled body. The stranger's brown eyes gleamed through the gap in his mask. Behind him, three more similarly dressed bandits spilled into the room holding their own bamboo staves. The leader's eyes zeroed in on the shattered vase on the work table before flicking to Harley and Qing across the room. His eyes widened slightly as they rested on Qing before narrowing once more.

'Give us the portion bearing the mark of Tiān Àn Jìn,' the man demanded as the three men behind him fanned out and began moving slowly around the skylight in the floor towards them. Darting a glance at Qing beside him, Harley saw her gaze sharpen at the mention of the mystical potter's name.

'Surrender the piece without struggle,' the man continued, 'and we will vanish from your lives like smoke. Tell Ray Spark he did Grandmaster Pang a great disservice in sending the Qing Long vase to the house of his greatest rival. It will not be forgotten.'

Qing shook her head curtly, and the leader cast his bamboo staff away in a gesture of disgust.

His stance changed, and his hands curled into hooks, the right one higher than the left. Without hesitation, the three other men did the same, their stances lowering, their steps quickening to mimic the movements of...

Harley tilted his head to one side. 'A monkey? Is that what they're doing? And what's with the hands?' He made exaggerated hooks in the air with his own hands and Garstang groaned from the floor near the stairs, 'They are masters of the Northern Praying Mantis kung fu style – go! Before they take out your eyes and grapple your heads straight off your necks!'

Ignoring Harley with his sticky-up hair, badly fitting clothes and wild-eyed air, the leader of the men made his way directly across the room to Qing. He loomed over her threateningly as his men took up position around the room behind him; the three of them blocked off any hope of access to the staircase. The lead bandit snapped his hands from claws into two stiff blade shapes, thumbs tucked in against his palms, right hand raised at the level of Qing's exposed jaw, left hand protecting his centre line, ready to chop her down at a moment's notice.

As Qing glared up at the man defiantly, he snarled at her, '*Gěi wǒ.*' The fingers of his right hand twitched in an attitude of *give it here* in case his words weren't clear enough.

Across the room, Garstang wheezed painfully from where he was lying on his back on the floor. 'Give him the mark, child. Chiu Chiu Pang is not to be trifled with.'

Qing shook her head again, and the man took a step back in surprise. The girl's eyes had turned black with fury.

'You're in for it now, mate,' Harley murmured, almost to himself.

The girl sagged suddenly, as if she were about to fall sideways to the ground, causing the man to lower his guard, before she crouched low and swept the man off his feet with her non-weight-bearing foot. The man clipped his head on the edge of a nearby work table as he fell, then lay still on the wooden floor. The three remaining bandits took a step backwards, looking at each other uncertainly.

'*Lóng yǒu sōu gǔ zhí fǎ,*' Qing hissed. 'Dragon defeats mantis.'

Harley was gobsmacked. He was still standing in exactly the same position – between Qing and the jade goddess, with the air of a stunned mullet – while Qing was already leaping across the fallen man's body and running in the direction of the next nearest brute.

The masked bandit retreated several steps, abandoning his praying mantis–style claws and extending his arms as if he wanted to bear-hug the small girl into submission. Before he could close his arms around her, though, Qing ducked and grabbed hold of one of the man's wrists, pulling down on it to upset his balance. As the man rocked forward, Qing pressed down, hard, on a point near his inner elbow with two bent fingers of her free hand. The man cried out in pain and, still latched on to his arm, Qing pivoted slightly and followed the sharp stab to his pressure point with a short action roundhouse kick to the lower ribs. The man gagged and fell forward and Qing changed her stance again, pushing the already off-balance man into the edge of a nearby work table. Multiple pieces of pottery fell to the floor with a shattering crash. Using the man's own falling weight against him, Qing pivoted her whole body one last time and pulled his arm back with a sharp motion. Harley could hear it pop right out of the man's shoulder just before the man fell to the ground, shrieking and rolling around beneath the table in agony, his arm at an unnatural angle.

The remaining two brutes finally sprang into motion together with wild eyes, their leading legs kicking out, their hands moving from left to right along a sinuous, hypnotic curve, as if grappling at invisible lines of force. Their stances altered again, hands curved once more into mantis claws as they trapped the girl between them in the centre of the glass skylight set into the floor. They would not make the same mistake as their fallen colleagues – it was clear that the girl possessed combat techniques in a style they did not recognise, but of a standard to pose them some danger.

She'd been lucky, but it was curtains, Harley felt sure. They were going to gouge her into submission with their lethal, pointed fingers. No kid could take on two grown men with the ability to turn into giant praying mantises at the drop of a hat. It was so unfair.

He cried out, 'Qing, please, *give them the piece.*'

The room went icy. Qing's hands started to

weave through the air between both men, her fingers like blades, then like fists, then back again, pulling at the air around her, pushing at the air around her, until the men seemed near hypnotised by the strange movements.

'*Qì shǒu*,' one of them muttered uneasily to the other, their own hands up now like deflecting blades. They stepped forward together, their leading hands testing the air so that Qing was forced to duck and weave around their clawlike jabs and feints.

The moment one of the men's raised forearms made contact with Qing's there was a *crack* of static electricity so loud and visible that the man fell to the floor with a howl, shuddering for a moment before going still.

Qing swivelled in the direction of the only man still on his feet, and he hesitated before running at her with a warlike cry, his leading fist directed straight at her small face. As she sidestepped his fist, she deflected it with one sharply raised elbow, the energy of her entire small form concentrated in the block. At her touch, the man let out a sharp cry of his own and fell to the floor, juddering on the ground as if he were in the grip of a terrible fit before he, too, went still.

Qing didn't hesitate, turning and flapping her billowing sleeves at Harley to run towards the jade statue of Guan Yin. They'd almost made it around the body of the stone goddess when a gunshot rang out, freezing them in their tracks. They swivelled around to see Chiu Chiu Pang's fifth man with Garstang J. Runyon's forgotten black handgun gripped in his right hand.

'Last chance to get out with your lives, children,' he hissed. 'The piece. Leave it at Guan Yin's feet or you all die.' He pointed the muzzle at Garstang's slumped, grey-faced form on the floor, then at the two of them.

Qing said – in the strangely resonant voice that Harley was only just getting used to hearing – 'Free old man first.' She pointed at the slumped form of the antiques dealer on the floor. When the masked bandit with the gun looked down at the old man by his feet, Qing drove an elbow into Harley's stomach so hard that he almost retched. But he got the message, and backed away silently towards the jade statue.

The man with the gun kicked the old man hard in the leg to indicate he was no longer necessary to proceedings. Instead of letting out the howl he so desperately wanted to, Garstang J. Runyon shot the two children an apologetic look, rolled over painfully onto his hands and knees and began crawling away to safety. While the gunman, laughing heartily, watched the old man leave at the pace of a wounded turtle, Harley backed past the right shoulder of the jade goddess and so did Qing.

Still laughing, the bandit with the gun turned to face them. 'The piece,' he reminded them menacingly, his laughter dying. The man extended his gun arm and began walking across the room towards them.

In response, Qing lowered her centre of gravity in the way that Harley had come to view as *trouble*, and crossed her wrists downwards before her as if there were a line running through the centre of her body, her wrists passing through that line.

'*Lěng*,' she barked in a way that sent shivers down Harley's spine. The word had seemed to bounce off all the exposed wooden rafters of the workroom.

The man paused in his forward progress, sniggering, '*Sudden*? Hardly.'

Qing ignored him and changed her guard so that both her arms were facing up, her wrists crossed just beneath her chin, the backs of her hands framing her face, and uttered the word, '*Tán.*'

The man's expression shifted into one of bored impatience. 'To spring?' he yawned. 'You're just standing there wasting my time. *The piece*, girl.'

Qing changed her guard again so that her crossed wrists jutted out to her right. '*Kuài,*' she snapped.

'My bullet will be *faster*,' the man retorted stepping forward again.

Qing changed her guard so that her crossed wrists and inward-facing hands covered her face from the right. '*Yìng,*' she roared.

'Hardness?' the man laughed, stopping mere metres away from Qing now, the right shoulder of the jade goddess the only thing disturbing the air between them. 'Flesh can never match the hardness of steel, the hardness of jade. You have no hope of defeating me.'

Qing turned her crossed guard so that this time it protected her left side at waist level. '*Ruǎn,*' she murmured.

'This is not the time to *relax* and *be fluid*,' the man said, raising the muzzle of his gun so that it was pointing directly at Qing's face.

Harley's skin went icy with fear. 'Qing!' he pleaded hoarsely from behind her.

The girl calmly finished the form she'd been sketching in the air so that her crossed wrists and inward-facing palms covered her face again, this time from the left. '*Qiǎo.*'

'Skilful?' the man snorted. 'All you've shown me is a simple form of centre line defence, fit only for small children. Is that the best you can do to protect your upper gate, your middle gate, your lower gate? Which one should I shoot at first, little girl?'

'*Jin!*' Qing roared suddenly and her wrists uncrossed so quickly Harley barely caught the change. She pushed her bladed hands outwards towards the man's face then pushed at the air sideways then forward again in the direction of the bandit, and the jade goddess ... *began to move.*

As the statue came off its wooden stand and began to glide then topple towards the gunman, he yelled out and fired. But it was true – no flesh was harder than jade, and jade was an element more inflexible than steel. As the gunman, cursing and spitting in Chinese, grappled with the heavy statue before it could crush him into the ground,

Qing turned, grabbed Harley by the wrist and ran towards the small steel door in the wall that the fallen goddess had once concealed.

As the two of them strained to pull open the rusted vertical floor and ceiling bolts that held the door closed, the gunman – still struggling to push the leaning statue off him – fired wildly in their direction. As the air went icy in the way Harley had come to associate with unseen power, the door opened, revealing a dark, musty concrete stairwell and a short flight of stairs that led up to the roof.

Qing ran up the claustrophobic set of stairs in near total darkness as Harley stumbled along behind her, missing the edges of stairs and tripping and falling over his own feet.

When she reached the top, she screamed, '*Kāi!*' and it seemed that the simple power of her voice made a door fly outwards to reveal a dirty concrete rooftop with nothing on it but a rickety TV antenna, the outline of the big glass skylight, and no way down.

'There's no fire escape!' Harley yelled, galloping all over the roof like a mad thing. 'We're trapped!'

He and Qing heard the statue of the Goddess of Mercy crash to the wooden floor below. Harley's heart was in his throat, then his mouth, as the gunman emerged onto the roof at a run, still wielding his gun. He stopped in his tracks as somewhere nearby sirens shrilled, growing louder as they drew closer.

Qing and Harley backed as far away as they could from the gunman and looked down the back edge of the building. This was not a movie. There was no conveniently placed garbage skip down below filled with large pieces of soft foam to land on. It was an empty alley lined with cobblestones, broken glass and old spew. That was it.

'The piece!' the gunman roared.

Qing took it out of her tunic and held it up high above her head, the mark facing outwards, as if she were going to smash it to pieces.

'No!' the gunman exclaimed. 'What are you doing? Do you know how much that is worth?'

Still holding the mark to the sky, Qing shouted, '*Dài lái fēngbào!*'

As her words died away, the sky lit up from end to end, ablaze with sheet lightning, illuminating every rooftop and building for miles around.

The energy in the air raised the hair on all their heads so that strands floated about them weirdly.

In that one frozen moment, it seemed they could see and know each other perfectly; that, in fact, they could see what things were made of – every mote of dust, every speck of paint and rust and dirt and energy that made up everything – they could somehow see it and *be* it. It was in them, it ran through them. *Power coursed like a river between them all.* The masked bandit dropped his gun, looking about him in awe, clutching at motes and streamers of light in the air.

Then the lightning was gone as abruptly as it appeared and the darkness was rent only by thunder louder than anything Harley had ever heard. It seemed to be going off like cannons inside his head. He doubled over, clutching his ears, wanting it to stop before his body turned inside out. The time his mum had taken him to see fireworks exploding over the river, one New Year's Eve, had nothing on this noise. *It's a sound that could tear you apart*, Harley thought. If it didn't stop soon, he would probably die.

In the heartbeat after the thunder finally rolled away, Qing said again, almost to herself, '*Dài lái fēngbào.*'

I bring the storm.

Harley, almost deaf and blind from the thunder and the lightning, only saw her lips moving.

Then the rain came down like a curtain, and seemed to obliterate the world.

Chapter 7

Harley was drowning standing up. That's what it felt like.

All he could see, hear, feel, breathe, was rain.

When he tried to yell out Qing's name, water filled his mouth and he began to choke. Then he felt her small hand grasp him by the collar of his awful old jacket like a claw and jerk him off his feet, and he was *falling with the rain*.

Falling and yelling.

Right off the back of the building.

The pressure on his collar suddenly eased and Harley landed on the ground at a stumbling run, almost sprawling on his face in the rain-slick, spew-slick alley at the back of Antediluvian House. There was the slimy, crunchy, solid feel of glass-littered cobblestones under his feet as Qing ran past him, dragging him with her by his sleeve as she raced out of the alley. As they rounded the back of a dumpling restaurant, they saw through the torrential downpour that Chinatown was filled with the pulsing red and blue lights of emergency vehicles. But instead of turning right and going towards the lights, Qing turned left swiftly before turning left again up a dog-legged alley and they were out of Chinatown and into an area of the city filled with offices and restaurants, cafes and shops.

She stopped running, settling into a fast walk. She didn't exactly hurry along the footpath, but she covered more ground than Harley could believe in a very short space of time, and he had to trot to keep up with her.

People in rain-splattered clothes were taking shelter from the sudden downpour everywhere, under shop awnings and inside the lobbies of buildings, their faces visible behind the streaming glass. Hurrying along behind Qing, it suddenly occurred to Harley – who was soaked right down into his squelching sneakers – that she was perfectly dry. From the hem of her billowing gold skirt up to the crown of her sleek black hair, Qing was untouched by the rain that poured down between the buildings.

The storm stopped abruptly at the exact moment Harley's special phone began to ring, quivering violently inside the pocket of his jacket. Qing turned and arched an eyebrow at Harley enquiringly as if to say, *Aren't you going to answer that?*

The people inside the office building closest to where Qing and Harley had stopped on the pavement stared through the glass at the kid in the loud bomber jacket with the knees almost worn through his jeans, standing next to a girl in a luminous, Chinese-style ball gown outfit straight out of an old painting. Harley turned his back on all the curious faces and fumbled his phone out of his pocket, pressing his thumb to the small camera icon that had appeared on the screen.

Ray Spark's features suddenly flooded into view and he was already shouting, 'Schumacher's ETA is fifty-eight seconds. Got that? Get in the car and stay down, do you hear me? Down on the floor in case Pang's still got gunmen on the rooftops!'

Harley knew for a fact that Pang still had at least one gunman on a rooftop because somehow, they'd left him up there. But Harley didn't mention this to his dad, or the whole thing about how he and Qing might just have broken a law of gravity, because Ray looked frantic enough as it was.

Qing peered down into the phone with interest, and Ray blinked as he caught sight of her, immediately taking in the bright ring of blue around the girl's dark eyes and the hand-embroidered gold and azure dragon twining around the collar of her (undoubtedly highly valuable) silk tunic because he was trained to see little details like that in a few seconds flat. In any museum job, Ray was the guy who could work out where the most valuable pieces in the place were, in one sweeping glance. He possessed both a valuer's eye and an assassin's reflexes, both skills that were invaluable in his line of work. A line of work Delia and Harley hardly knew about.

'Schumacher's pulling up right beside you now,' Ray snapped, Harley wondering in bewilderment how on earth his dad could know that from his vantage point in a place called Buda. 'I'll call you again when you're at a more secure location.'

Then the small silver phone went dead in Harley's hand and a sleek black sports car with dark-tinted windows drew up at the kerb beside them and Ray's helper Schumacher (Harley had never been exactly sure what he 'helped' with) threw the front passenger door open from the inside, shouting, '*Kleine freunde! Schnell! Schnell!*'

Although Schumacher looked like the bass player for a death metal band with his lank, shoulder-length blond hair, broken nose and rangy build, Qing scooped her voluminous skirts up with one hand and slid gracefully into the front seat without hesitation. Harley scrambled into the back, only just managing not to shut the door on his foot before Schumacher floored the accelerator and bore them away.

They were pulling into an enormous aircraft hangar at a private airfield on the outskirts of the international airport when Harley's phone rang again. As he pressed his thumb onto the camera icon in answer, Harley stared up through Schumacher's wraparound windscreen at a huge, gleaming jet parked smack bang in the middle of the hangar. It had twin engines and eleven windows along each side and the front door near the pilot's cockpit was open, with gold-carpeted stairs leading down to them invitingly. All the lights were on inside the plane. It was the most beautiful aircraft Harley had ever seen.

'Harls?' his dad said sharply out of the device in Harley's palm. 'Over here, mate.' Harley ripped his gaze away from the gleaming jet and looked down at his dad's face.

Schumacher turned the engine off, flicking on the car's interior lights, and he and Qing turned to look at Harley expectantly.

Harley blinked at the sand dunes now framing Ray Spark's features. 'Are you standing in a *desert*, Dad? What on earth is going on?'

'I need you to get on that plane, son,' Ray replied hurriedly. 'I can answer all your questions later when you touch down. Chiu Chiu Pang has put a price on your heads and effectively declared war on me and my business, ah, interests.' Ray's eyes darted about as if he were trying to see around the insides of Schumacher's car. 'He's also put out word that the person who can bring him the dragon vase currently in the possession of the ridiculously wealthy Quek family of Balestier Road, Singapore, within the next forty-eight hours will earn a bounty of ten million dollars payable in cash, diamonds, camels or anything "the finder" likes.'

Schumacher's mouth fell open. 'It will be the bloodbath, boss,' he said from the driver's seat in his thick Bavarian accent. 'Such a handsome bounty.'

Ray nodded grimly. 'The Quek vase – the only other known vase in existence in the series you showed me, Harls – is worth upwards of sixty-six million *pounds*, boys, so ten million dollars' worth of camels, or whatever, would be cheap at twice the price. And he's put the same bounty on the two of you,' Ray added grimly, 'for insulting his honour. Five apiece, or ten mill for the pair of you dead or alive, but preferably dead because it's just neater and will hurt me more. That's a total prize pool of twenty million dollars floating in the breeze, waiting for someone to grab hold of it. Sources are telling me that even if I deliver the vase to Grandmaster Pang myself, you two still might not be safe because he's not a forgiving man! What have you got yourself mixed up in, son?'

Harley quickly caught his dad up on all the things that had happened since he'd liberated the old vase off the footpath outside Hammonds the Auctioneers on a whim. He knew what he was saying sounded utterly fantastical, but Ray's expression did not change one iota as he listened; Harley knew Ray's mind was processing the hard facts, the way he'd trained himself to do, and discounting the rest.

After Harley finished his breathless recount of the scene on the roof of Antediluvian House (*'Our hair was doing something like out of* The Matrix, *Dad!'*) all Ray observed was, 'If what you're saying is true – that's no ordinary girl, Harls.'

'You're telling me,' Harley said, staring at Qing through the gap between the two front seats; her return gaze was fierce and unblinking. Harley had come to think of the piercing look she was giving him as her *thinking face*. 'The rain can't touch her and she might have read the entire contents of the State Library in one night,' Harley added. 'Like, last night she couldn't speak English, and, and now... she kind of *can*.'

'Mmmm,' was all Ray said, as if he heard things like this every day of his life.

At that moment, a small flashing camera icon appeared at the top right of the screen of Harley's phone. It had the word *Mum* written under it in bright, danger-warning red.

'It's Mum!' Harley's voice rose to an anxious squeak. 'What do I do? Whatever do I say?'

'Put her on,' Ray said a touch squeakily himself. 'This concerns her too.'

Delia had told Harley very, very firmly (in no uncertain terms) after Ray had moved out with his one meagre bag of belongings that she never wanted to speak to Harley's dad ever again. And she'd pretty much stuck to those guns for the last eight years.

'You know this is breaching Mum's rule,' Harley said nervously, 'about the whole speaking and contact thing. She's going to scream at us.'

'Put her on,' Ray sighed.

As soon as Harley pressed the flashing icon, the screen broke up into two halves and Delia screeched loud enough to distort the audio, making both Ray and Harley wince and cower at the same time. 'Where have you taken our boy, Ray Patrick Spark? He's already missed one whole day of school. *One whole day.* Every grown adult who emerged out of that building you told him to go to – and I clearly watched Harley walk into it – *denies he was ever there.*

This has something to do with you, Ray, I know it does. It's all your fault.'

Delia appeared to be sitting in the back of an ambulance with a bandage bound tightly around her forehead at a rakish angle. Her shiny black hair puffed out over the top of it muffin-style. She was also sporting a huge black eye and a cut lip. 'You bring him back home this instant!' Her face loomed large in the screen as she leant forward and searched her son's face. 'I was so worried, Harley. If something ever happened to you ...' Her big brown eyes filled with sudden tears.

Ray gazed at Delia with a mix of hopeless adoration and resignation on his face, which made his usually hard-edged features look younger and softer. 'That's the whole problem, Delia. Harley can't go home yet, and neither can you. There are over four hundred styles of Chinese martial art and Chiu Chiu Pang is a grandmaster of at least fifty-six of them. He knows where you live. He'll be watching your place and my place, Harley's school. You need to stay with friends, not family – at least until I tell you it's safe to go home. Harley will be with me. *I won't let anything happen to him.* You have my word on that. It's just that we need to fix things so that you can go home again, and everything goes back to normal. Just tell his school, I dunno, that I've taken him for an extended, um, educational camping trip.'

Inside the car, Schumacher and Harley exchanged glances; the camping trip was likely to be very extended, and involve a large private jet.

'This is the second and very last time I let you ruin our lives, Ray Spark!' Delia's features were pale with fear and anger, but she knew Ray well enough to understand from his tone of voice that this was one of those *life and death* moments he'd warned Harley about only weeks earlier. Delia sensed this was worse than the time the police had stormed their home and turned their lives upside down. She searched Harley's face again. 'You stick like glue to your dad and come home as soon as you can, love, all right? Learn as much as you can on your "camping trip", and if you pick up some useful skills along the way, it won't be a complete waste.'

Delia's eyes darted around the interior of Schumacher's car, too, just as Ray's had earlier. 'Can you put her on?' Delia said abruptly.

Surprised, Harley handed the phone across to Qing in the front seat, who held it cupped in both her hands like a rare and fragile flower. She bent her face over the screen and said quietly, 'Yes, *Mā ma* Delia?'

She looked, with interest, from Ray's face to Delia's on the screen, both so very different.

'Qing, love, Harley needs your help now,' Delia said as Harley groaned, 'Mum!' from the back seat.

Delia ignored her son, continuing to address Qing. 'I know you can do things, special things. The kinds of things my grandfather – Harley's great-grandpa – used to talk about. Please do what you can to keep him safe—'

'*Mum!*'

'Quiet, Harley dear, Qing and I are having a word,' Delia continued pleasantly. 'Girls are more mature, it's been scientifically proven. Make sure he eats, pet, and that he calls home regularly—'

'Mum, I'm right here—'

'Delia—'

'I'm not speaking to you, Ray Spark—'

'*Mum!*'

Qing laughed suddenly, a rippling sound filled with genuine delight, and it was so unexpected that the three arguing Sparks fell silent in surprise.

'You give me back *life*, Spark family,' Qing replied in her low, resonant voice. 'We have – how do you say? – *guānxi* now. Connection.' She screwed up her face, trying to get the right words out. '*Trust*. The Children of the Dragon…' for a moment Qing looked very sad, but then the look passed, '…will do all they can to preserve you.'

Delia nodded grimly, knowing it would have to do.

Ray added, 'I'm meeting Harley straight off the plane in Singapore, Delia. Schumacher's got him until then and you know Schumacher's a straight-up guy—'

'Yes, *hallo*, yoo-hoo,' Schumacher interjected quickly from the side. 'Mrs Spark, I am very straight-up, you know this.'

'Singapore?' Delia yelped in horror. 'You mean you aren't already *together*?'

'Eight hours,' Ray cajoled, 'that's all that's separating me from Harley, Deels. I'm headed there right now. I'll be there waiting for him. It's a, uh, relatively easy fix, this thing me and the kids have to do together. Piece of cake. We'll call you as soon as we're all together, all right?'

Then Ray did something to the phone from

wherever he was standing in a desert in Qatar, and the three-way connection went dead.

☞

Schumacher showed them all over the plane while the two pilots remained discreetly locked behind the cockpit doors at the front. All Schumacher said was, 'It's better if they don't see you. See me? Is okay. If someone asks them, *Wo sind die kinder?*' – when Schumacher got a bit excited, his German kept bursting out – 'the pilots, they can shrug and say, hand on the heart, *What children? We have seen no children here.*'

Everything was fascinating to Qing, who wanted to touch and prod every surface of the aeroplane. But it was pretty fascinating to Harley, too, because all the interior of the plane contained was a long, oval conference table topped with flame walnut wood panelling, surrounded by twelve comfy-looking leather armchairs – one at each end, five on either side – and a bathroom that featured a washbasin and a full-sized spa with real gold taps. Long cupboards, also in flame walnut, ran along either side of the plane beneath the windows. Having a meeting and then having a spa, or having a spa first and then a business meeting, was something Harley had never even contemplated. Adults were weird.

'This is the strangest aeroplane I've ever seen,' he whistled from where he was standing at the head of the meeting table; the locked cockpit door at his back, the soft gold carpet almost swallowing his damp, smelly sneakers.

'It is even better below the decks!' Schumacher crowed, opening two broad cupboard doors just outside the bathroom. 'Follow me! Tight squeeze for me; not so much for you!'

Qing and Harley watched as Schumacher slid sideways into the empty cupboard bum-first, before tucking his knees against his chest and rolling onto his back.

Then he *disappeared*.

Qing blinked.

Harley sprinted across the cabin, kneeling to look into the cupboard where Schumacher had just vanished, running his hands along the empty shelving. Schumacher might never have been there but for his muffled voice crying, 'Join me!' floating up to them from somewhere under the cupboard floor.

Qing knelt too, astonishment on her face, pressing down on the apparently solid wood, which didn't budge a millimetre. She stuck her head in the cupboard to see how the big German had done it.

'How?' Harley yelled back, feeling foolish. 'How do we do that?'

'Lie on your back,' Schumacher bellowed up. 'There is a catch where one panel meets another, near the roof. *Deine zehen*, your toes, you know? Just a tiny wiggle, you must feel it—'

Qing got into the cupboard, rolling up into a ball and feeling with one of her small slippered feet around the ceiling of the enclosed space. With a look of complete surprise, she dropped downwards, and the floor rose smoothly back up.

'Okay?' Harley heard Schumacher roar jovially. '*Woo!* Am I right?'

'Woo!' Qing replied, with laughter in her voice.

There was a hollow knock on the false floor of the cupboard. '*Kommst du*, Harley?'

Taking a deep breath, Harley shoved his bum into the cupboard, flipped over onto his back and toed the catch.

He fell so fast his stomach filled with butterflies.

Chapter 8

When he threw himself out of the fake cupboard, which was already rising back towards the plush interior of the plane, Harley found himself in a cold, vast, dim space which ran the entire length of the jet. Harley blinked in astonishment as he scanned what had to be the cargo hold. The false cupboard had deposited them near the tail end, and between where they were standing and the nose of the plane, the hold was crammed full of dark, oddly-shaped things.

Harley did a double take. 'Are those all ... musical instruments?' he asked Schumacher, who was standing a little hunched over because of his great height. Harley hadn't known what to expect. Maybe a planeload of liberated Van Gogh or Picasso paintings, given the way Delia was always muttering darkly about Ray's *business interests*. There wasn't a sniff of antique bric-à-brac or artwork to be seen down here, and Harley felt a burst of relief. Maybe his mum had been wrong about his dad all along.

Around them were stacked large cardboard boxes which bore labels like *Mixed Recorders* or *Flutes/Piccolos*. Near the single cargo door at the midpoint of the hold was a cluster of six very large kettledrums, each standing on sturdy legs set into a big brass ring that went around the belly of each drum. There were a couple of upright pianos, one on either side of the hold near the front of the plane, and a couple of double basses in hard cases sitting flat on the floor at the plane's nose-end. Around the prone double basses were at least a dozen cello cases resting on their sides. Strong black webbing held almost everything in position except for the pianos, which were strapped around their tops to the side walls. There wasn't much space to walk around between the pinned-down cargo.

'I show you something,' Schumacher said, beckoning them towards one of the pianos.

The three of them squeezed past a box marked *Tiger Bassoons*, then another marked *French Horns* and stared at the piano, which was a glossy black with gold trim and a German-sounding name: *Källtewelle*. 'My uncle,' Schumacher said proudly, tapping the side of his nose, 'he makes them special.'

Schumacher lifted the lid of the piano and Qing and Harley stood on tiptoe to see inside. 'Good steel frame, see?' Schumacher added, plucking at one of the golden piano strings. 'Very sturdy. Last forever.'

He lifted the fallboard that covered the piano's keys and grinned. 'Play it,' he urged them.

Harley reached forward and pressed one of the splendid high-gloss ivory keys with his index finger, but no sound came out. Puzzled, he placed both his hands on the keyboard and crashed them up and down as if he were Beethoven, but the piano remained completely silent. There was just a dead-sounding thump each time he pressed down on the keyboard.

Qing looked at Schumacher enquiringly, and Schumacher folded his lanky frame onto the ground beneath the keyboard, beckoning them to do the same. As they knelt by the pedals of the piano, Schumacher slid open a secret panel located just above the pedals that was controlled by a tiny catch, much like the one inside the false cupboard above their heads. Harley saw that the empty space was big enough to hold a person, sitting scrunched up with their knees under their chin. 'A good hiding spot, *ja*?' Schumacher said happily.

'Do they both do that?' Harley gestured at the other piano across the hold.

Schumacher shook his head. 'Only this one. In case anyone is asking, the other one plays like a dream. And follow me now...'

They squeezed past a couple of boxes marked *Triangles & Misc. Beaters* and moved towards the two double bass cases that were flat on the ground near the nose of the plane. They were hard to see among all the boxes and cellos, but strangely, one of them wasn't strapped down. 'This one,' Schumacher announced, waving at the double bass case furthest from the cargo door, 'is empty. Also good for the hiding.'

He stepped carefully over the cargo of webbed cello cases and bent down, opening the special black double bass case by flipping the catches on the side. Its interior was also marked with the gold *Källtewelle* maker's label. Schumacher ran his hand across the fuzzy maroon pile inside the empty case and indicated a couple of very ingenious breathing holes carved into the area near the lid hinges that weren't readily discernible from the outside of the case. 'Very comfortable for you, *ja?*' he said to Qing. 'I think a good fit.'

Schumacher stood and pointed at the kettle drums by the cargo hold door, indicating the tripod arrangement that held each of them up. 'Two of them also can be accessed from beneath, but for you, Harley, very tight squeeze, I am thinking. Not the best choice.' He pointed at a box in a narrow space near the nose of the plane. 'That one is only half full of tambourines, but I do not recommend it. The slightest movement may be heard, I am thinking. And you will need to be very quiet when we land, you understand? Customs must be seeing only musical instruments, nothing else.'

Qing and Harley nodded solemnly in under-standing. 'There's no way back up into the plane from here,' Schumacher said as he led them towards the cargo hold door and released it, helping them back onto the brushed concrete floor of the hangar before closing the door behind them. 'Once you are down, you are down. And you must be like the mice.'

As they filed back up the front stairs of the plane, he asked, 'Any questions, *kinder*?'

Harley's jaw dropped as Qing answered in what sounded like German, '*Haben sie fisch oder wasser?*' and Schumacher threw up his large hands in delight. He started foraging in the supply cabinets along the right side of the plane for whatever Qing had asked for – Harley guessed either *fish* or *water*. Empires had risen and fallen since she'd last eaten, and she was starving and thirsty after the day's shenanigans.

The jet took off not long after. While Qing ate tin after tin of tuna with a cocktail fork and practised with Schumacher the nineteenth-century-era German phrases she'd picked up from books inside the State Library, Harley threw his legs over one arm of the chairman's seat at the head of the board table, and slept with his head thrown back and his mouth wide open.

Harley woke abruptly when the plane encountered heavy turbulence. Schumacher was asleep with his face on the meeting table and his pale death-metal hair spread out everywhere, but Qing was wide awake, surrounded by a mountain of empty tuna tins and bottles of water. She was staring out one of the windows across the cabin and looked terribly sad.

Harley yawned, stretched and sat up. 'What's wrong?' he asked Qing without thinking. Asking a girl what was wrong was usually trouble, but Qing wasn't like any girl he had ever met before, so the words came out before he could suck them back in.

She didn't answer right away, and she didn't look away from the window at Harley. If anything, the question made Qing look sadder. When it seemed like she would ignore him completely, she finally replied so quietly that he had to strain to hear her.

'There is no one – out there,' she pointed out the window, which was streaming with thin rivulets of rain, 'like me.'

'We're all different,' Harley said encouragingly. 'That's what Mum always tells me, anyway, when Reggie Brandis has been trying to shove my head down a toilet again. There's no one like any of us, if you look at it that way. Nothing to feel glum about! We're all *islands*, according to my teacher Miss Harris.'

Qing turned to look at Harley and the ring

around her black irises seemed blue with a kind of actualised sorrow. She peered again into the dark turbulence outside as the whole aircraft gave an awkward lurch and roll that almost pitched a now-groaning Schumacher out of his seat. Harley clutched desperately at the armrests of his own chair so that he wouldn't hit the carpet on his bum.

'Out there,' Qing said in frustration, trying to make Harley understand, 'the sky is … empty.'

Harley's eyes widened. 'You mean, it didn't used to be?'

Qing shook her head. 'Before there were machines like this,' her eyes darted around the interior of the jet, '*we* were there. Where have we gone?'

Harley was opening his mouth to pepper her with questions when Schumacher abruptly sat straight up and scooped his lank locks off his face.

'Righto,' he said looking from Qing to Harley, rubbing the sleep out of his ice-blue eyes, 'time to get in the cupboard, *kinder.*'

In the hold, Harley could feel the strong g-forces of their descent. They vibrated up through the steel floor into his shoes and then into his bones. His teeth were chattering as he picked his way towards the piano with the false door at the base. Qing had gone straight for the double bass case with the air holes. They exchanged looks before disappearing inside their respective hiding places.

The landing was bumpy and uncomfortable. Secreted inside the piano, Harley bit his tongue when the wheels of the plane hit the ground. The iron taste of his own blood filled his mouth disgustingly as the aircraft coasted swiftly to a stop. Not long after, the cargo door opened and they heard Schumacher say in his loud, jolly Bavarian voice, 'A very uneventful trip, my friend, nothing to report.'

A new voice replied dryly, 'Although I must say, *my friend*, that you ate a lot of tuna for such a short trip! More than two tins per hour, if I am not mistaken, given the favourable tailwind on your journey.'

'I was very hungry,' Schumacher replied as the two men's footsteps began to echo around the hold. 'Tuna is my favourite food.'

'The passenger manifest lists only your name, it is true. But *seventeen* tins of sandwich tuna in olive oil?' the stranger replied doubtfully.

Inside their hiding places, Qing and Harley

tensed at the scepticism in the customs official's voice, sensing trouble.

'I assure you,' Schumacher said without hesitation, 'I most certainly am the only passenger aboard this plane. And I most certainly ate all of that tuna. I *love* tuna. I *dream* about tuna when I am not eating tuna. It is the food of the brain.'

'Mmmmmm,' the other man replied as he took a few more steps forward into the hold, then stopped. 'You say these instruments are all bound for a music shop in the suburb of Novena?'

'Yes, sir,' Schumacher replied, sounding less jolly as the man resumed walking into the hold, evidently looking around. 'I explained all this to your colleague, Mr Low, when I called ahead to tell him of our arrival date.'

'Mr Low is indisposed today,' the other man replied sternly. 'I am his supervisor. This seems like a lot of instruments for one shop to order.'

Harley stopped breathing as a set of heavy knuckles knocked on the lid of the very piano he was hiding in. He felt sure Schumacher had stopped breathing for a moment, too, because when Schumacher spoke again, his voice sounded high and funny.

There was a small creak and the cover on

Harley's keyboard began to open. Harley gritted his teeth together so hard that fresh blood welled in his mouth. If the supervisor tried to tinkle these ivories, he'd know for sure that something was even fishier than the empty tuna cans Qing had left behind upstairs.

Schumacher tore open the top of a box nearby and scooped up a handful of things that clinked wildly. 'For the *kinder*,' he said hastily. 'A local school has placed an order for hundreds of these triangles.'

The supervisor placed the fallboard gently back down but Harley didn't start breathing again until the two men's footsteps moved further away. 'Timpani from America, guitars from Andorra,' Schumacher recited quickly, 'violins and violas from an artisanal *violineri* in Venice, xylophones from Japan.' Harley could hear Schumacher frantically throwing open box lids all over the hold.

'What about those?' said the supervisor, stopping with a scuff of his shoes.

'The double basses?' Schumacher sounded scared and squeaky again.

'They are the same brand as the pianos,' the supervisor mused. '*Källtewelle*. In my experience, makers of fine pianos do not ordinarily also make stringed instruments. Open the cases, please.'

'Open the cases?' Schumacher sounded the most terrified Harley had ever heard him.

'Open the cases,' the other man repeated in a voice both deeply pleasant and deeply menacing.

In the echoing hold, Harley heard Schumacher shoot the catches on the first case and wheeze, 'See, the finest German maple wood, handcrafted in the forests of Bavaria, where I am coming from. Look at the flame pattern in the wood. So beautiful.'

'The other case,' the man insisted immediately, his voice dropping as he bent down to inspect the case that Qing had hidden in. 'See, the catches are already open. All you need to do, *my friend*, is lift the lid.'

Schumacher shuffled his feet in agony.

Harley thought his head would explode in fear as Schumacher finally lifted the lid. Both men made an exclamation of surprise and dismay.

'It's empty!' they both shouted at once.

Harley had been sweating into his clothes inside the piano's hot and stuffy hidey-hole, but their words made him go ice cold. Empty?

'How can this be?' Schumacher howled, looking around the hold as if the missing double bass had gotten up by itself and walked away.

The customs official noted the German's genuine surprise and anguish and reluctantly put his signature on the top page of the sheaf of customs documents on his clipboard. You couldn't stop a shipment that *didn't* conceal contraband even if it was, in fact, missing some legitimate bits. Still, it was clear from his face that the customs officer felt faintly cheated.

There was a long pause as the supervisor's gaze swept the entire contents of the cargo hold one more time. 'I should think that the folk at *Källtewelle* have fooled you out of one double bass, which is most irregular, but not irregular enough to stop you. You can tell your truck driver to take delivery now,' the man added.

But his words didn't give Harley or Schumacher much comfort. Where was Qing?

Schumacher and the driver of the truck loaded the instruments in silence, no doubt watched by the eagle-eyed customs official who could sense that something was off, but couldn't prove what it was. As the men loaded the piano holding Harley into the back of the truck, Harley heard Schumacher shout, 'Right, that's the last one!' before the tailgates slammed shut. Not long after the truck set off, Harley slid open the panel protecting his hiding place slightly, just to get some air.

The back of the truck was unbelievably hot because Singapore itself was hot and humid and filled with tropical vegetation smells Harley had never experienced before. He'd never been out of Australia until today. Inside the truck, the atmosphere seemed triply concentrated. He was sweltering inside his flannel shirt, jeans and heavy bomber jacket, but there was no space inside the piano to wiggle his jacket off. If Schumacher didn't stop the truck soon, he was going to sweat to death.

Harley's heart almost jumped out of his chest when the panel on the piano suddenly slid open the whole way. In the pitch-black darkness of the truck filled with tinkling, bonging, creaking instruments, he could make out two glowing golden eyes with black irises ringed in blue.

They're the eyes from the vase, Harley thought, actually cowering. The dragon's eyes he hadn't been able to look away from. The whole time he'd fooled himself into thinking she was just a kid in fancy dress, because that's what she looked like – a kid in fancy dress. But Qing was something *else* as well. Somehow she was two things at once, although he had no concrete proof of that either.

What *had* he got himself into?

'Where did you go?' Harley whispered, terrified, as the eyes continued to watch him steadily and unblinkingly, although what he really wanted to jabber was, *Don't eat me, don't eat me, don't eat me.*

Qing's laughter cut across the steady rumble of the truck's engine. 'You're safe. I just ate,' she reminded him, making his blood freeze all over again. 'And I only like to eat fish. The man did not see me – but I was there.'

A hand came forward in the darkness – a small, smooth, entirely human-style hand – and Qing helped Harley out of the piano. His whole lower body had gone to sleep and the blood rushing back into his feet, ankles and legs brought with it a painful cascade of pins and needles. They sat on the floor of the truck together, Harley's piano like a canopy over their heads, waiting for the hot, stuffy journey to end.

About ten minutes later, it felt like the truck was turning ponderously and heading downwards. If it was possible, the heat inside the truck was building, growing almost unbearable. Qing squeezed Harley's hand, somehow sensing his physical distress. 'I am feeling it is not much longer,' she murmured.

And she was right, because the truck braked to a stop and the doors were quickly thrown open. Harley shielded his eyes as a strong flashlight played across the back of the truck; he sensed that Qing met the light without blinking, even though they'd been sitting in absolute darkness for almost an hour.

'Qing!' Harley heard Schumacher exclaim. 'You are here! *Danke Gott.* You hid among the tambourines, *ja?*'

Qing shook her head, pulling Harley to his tingly feet.

'Somewhere else,' she replied, grinning. 'That was fun. I had forgotten how to do that.'

Schumacher – who was now wearing a grey removalist's jumpsuit – and Harley squinted at each other, unsure what she was talking about, which only made Qing grin more widely.

'Harls?' another voice said uncertainly.

Harley stumbled forward. 'Dad? *Dad!*'

Still half-blind, he almost fell off the back of the truck into his dad's waiting bear hug.

As his eyes cleared, Harley could see that the truck was in a dimly lit basement car park that smelled strongly of rotting fruit and diesel. The truck driver cleared his throat discreetly and busied himself engaging the hydraulic tailgate at the back of the truck.

While Qing waited for the tailgate to finish moving into place so that she could step down, Harley and Schumacher and his dad stood watching her. She was framed by cardboard boxes and instruments of all shapes and sizes, but she stood very straight – regal and immaculate, but wary. The heat and humidity weren't flattening her hair to her head the way they were doing to Harley; sweat wasn't streaming down her face and neck and armpits and spine like a river. That, even more than the weird golden glow of her eyes in the dim basement, told Harley she was something other than what she seemed.

Ray – also wearing a grey jumpsuit – raised his hand to help the girl step down the ramp, yelping as a strong blue spark of static electricity leapt between their clasped fingers. But Ray didn't let the girl's hand go until she had both feet on the floor.

'It means she likes you, Dad.' Harley smiled. 'This is Qing.'

Ray bowed his head as if he were meeting the Queen. 'I'm Harley's dad, Ray,' he said gently.

'Bāba Ray,' Qing replied, urgency in her low tone. 'I need you to help me get the Quek vase because – it is no vase.'

'It's a person,' Harley interjected, 'just like her.'

Ray shook his head, half in amusement, half in disbelief. He looked into Qing's small, angular face. 'A lot of people are after that vase at this point in time, young lady. I can't make any promises – there are things that need to be made right – but I do have a little plan I need to run past you two.'

He placed his hands carefully on the children's shoulders, half-bracing for an electrical charge to leap between the three of them.

'Schumacher,' Ray ordered, beckoning to his old friend and partner-in-crime, 'get in close, and listen up.'

Chapter 9

Ray explained that night had fallen and that they were all standing in a car park under a multilevel shopping centre an hour's drive from Balestier Road. The Quek mansion, Ray added, was the only colonial-era mansion left along the busy six-lane thoroughfare amid office buildings, shopping malls and hotels. It was a measure of the family's enormous wealth and influence that they still held a two-acre compound right in the heart of crowded Singapore. The Queks had been living there for almost a hundred and fifty years.

'So the mansion,' Ray continued hurriedly, 'is protected by a twenty-foot concrete and reinforced steel perimeter wall, a physical security team of two dozen men who rotate through each twelve-hour shift a dozen at a time and twenty-four-seven CCTV with multiple internal and exterior cams. From schematics of the house I managed to obtain once – dated from just before the significant renovation undertaken in nineteen ninety-four,' Harley wrinkled his nose; that was so far back it was just about *the olden days*, 'the entire east wing is likely to function as the Quek family's personal museum of rare Chinese artwork and artefacts, based on the building works that were intended for that area. The vase is likely to be in some kind of secure location in that part of the mansion.'

'It sounds impossible, boss,' Schumacher said glumly from over Ray's shoulder. 'We will never get inside without being seen, the four of us.'

'We're in luck today.' Ray smiled as another truck rumbled down the ramp towards them and parked nearby. The two truck drivers started to shift musical instruments from one truck to the other as the children and Schumacher continued to huddle around Ray. 'The entire Quek family flew to Hong Kong last week to watch a rugby match *en masse* with most of their security team. The mansion is empty of occupants. Even the two housekeepers and the gardener who live in outbuildings away from the main house aren't home – they've been given a few days off.'

Ray looked uncomfortable for a moment, then continued. 'Because only people in my, uh, specific line of work know about the bounty on the dragon vase, there are only *six* security guards on duty at the mansion at present; the rest are trailing the family around Hong Kong. 'Plus –' Ray tapped his nose in way that made Schumacher grin, 'security is going to find an order for a nice new *Källtewelle* in the housekeeping database. It won't really matter if we're seen – we're going to deliver a piano today, and a little bit more besides.'

They napped until just after sunrise, then Schumacher himself drove the delivery truck up out of the basement car park while Ray, Qing and Harley huddled in the back, now almost empty because most of the musical instruments had been removed.

'How did you get hold of the renovation plans for that house, Dad?' Harley asked as the three of them sat cross-legged in a circle on the steel floor of the truck beside the remaining *Källtewelle* piano (the one that played actual notes, not the special one with the hidey-hole), which had a hand cart with wheels wedged in below it now.

Ray's voice went a bit vague. 'I might have been researching a potential, ah, job at the Quek mansion just over twenty years ago. Around the time the family acquired the vase in the first place, actually. The job got called off.'

'What kind of job?' Harley said suspiciously.

Ray didn't answer Harley's question but said instead, 'The truck will be stopping shortly and I'm going to get out and sit beside Schumacher. When we reach the front of the mansion we'll make enough fuss to ensure you can get inside. Don't think about the cameras or it will slow you down – we'll draw the men away from the CCTV feeds and control room as much as we can. Just try your hardest to make sure you're not seen, and head straight for the ground floor of the east wing. You'll see a giant stone statue of a god standing guard at the door to the collection: flowing beard, frightening expression. On the plan we're talking floor-to-ceiling big – he's unmissable. The statue will provide a good hiding place for kids as skinny as you two. Just keep your heads down and I'll join you as soon as I can.'

'What about Schumacher?' Harley asked as Qing listened intently, a small frown pleating her brows.

'Schumacher's our way out,' Ray said shortly as their truck rumbled to a stop. 'You always have to have someone on the outside. It's one of my ground rules. No exceptions. Inside the mansion, it will be just the three of us.'

'No,' Qing insisted, shaking her head so fiercely her hair fell about her face, 'just *me*.'

'The Sparks have got your back,' Ray said firmly. 'We've come this far. And the Quek collection is legendary and a closely guarded secret. I want to see it. I want to see that *vase*. This may be my only chance, ever. I never thought it would come.'

'Dad, that vase is a *person*,' Harley reminded him, frowning.

'That vase,' Ray reminded him sternly, 'is our ticket out of this mess, Harls. Remember that.'

Qing and Harley exchanged troubled glances as Schumacher swung one of the back doors of the truck open.

Ray shielded his eyes from the hot, golden, early morning sunshine as Schumacher handed

Harley a small plastic bag with handles, containing some kind of pale green juice with a straw in it, a banana leaf full of heavenly smelling food, and a plastic fork. Qing shook her head when Schumacher offered her the same thing, so Ray, Schumacher and Harley wolfed their hot breakfasts down while Ray continued speaking.

'It's not far now,' he said, indicating a pile of felt blankets heaped up in the corner of the truck with his plastic fork. 'When the truck gets going again, I need you to get under the blankets, kids, and keep very still and quiet when the truck stops at the gate to the mansion.'

As Ray got to his feet, taking Harley's rubbish with him, he said to Qing, 'Will you recognise what you're looking for? There'll be no time to hesitate. We'll need to grab and go.'

She nodded. 'If the vase is there, I will find it,' she answered fiercely.

Ray nodded as he jumped out of the back of the truck. 'Blankets,' he reminded them as Schumacher handed Ray a grey cap that said *Courier* across the front. Schumacher slipped his own cap on his head before giving Qing and Harley a broad wink and slamming the door shut.

The truck only seemed to travel another few kilometres before it slowed to a stop again at the guardhouse outside the Quek mansion. Harley and Qing scrambled under the blankets, which felt unbearably heavy, hot and scratchy.

There were a couple of raised, enquiring voices from outside the vehicle and Harley heard Schumacher reply loudly in his bluff Bavarian accent, 'My friend, see for yourself!'

The back doors to the truck swung open and, beneath his heavy blanket, Harley froze as Schumacher knocked on the side of the piano. 'One fine German piano! As ordered.' He lifted the lid and bashed on the keys before placing it down again. 'See! Here are the papers!'

Harley almost fell asleep again in his blanket nest as the security guards argued with someone inside the compound on their walkie-talkies. The truck doors finally clanged shut and the truck started up, travelling very slowly up a raked gravel drive before it pulled to another stop and the engine cut out.

The back doors to the truck opened again and Harley heard his dad say, 'Where do you want it, sport? Don't have all day.'

Schumacher engaged the automated ramp at the

back of the truck while two new voices argued about the origin of the order.

Four guards, Harley ticked off in his head. That left only two, elsewhere in the grounds.

The big German started to whistle as he cheerfully began unloading the upright piano from the truck.

'Stop right there!' the third man shouted in frustration. 'No one authorised this!'

'I have the deadlines,' Schumacher said calmly, as he kept lowering the glossy black piano to the ground with the help of the handcart. 'You cannot be getting in the way of my deadlines.'

Harley heard the crunch of gravel as Schumacher wheeled the piano off the ramp and onto the gravel-covered drive.

'We have no record of an order for a piano,' the fourth guard insisted angrily. 'There is already a concert grand inside the house.'

'I think you will see that you do,' Schumacher said patiently, still whistling as he pulled the piano away from the truck. 'I shall take it around the side, seeing as how pianos cannot be travelling up front stairs.'

'Stop! Where are you going?' someone new shouted, running closer.

Five security guards, Harley said to himself. Man number six was probably watching all the action on a closed circuit TV somewhere inside.

'I cannot be taking this up the front stairs,' Schumacher repeated, as he kept dragging the piano away from the truck, drawing two of the security guards with him from the sound of their crunching footfalls. 'Call your supervisor,' Harley heard Schumacher yell cheerfully, his voice growing fainter and fainter.

'I will!' a man retorted fiercely.

The security man who remained demanded to see Ray's paperwork. 'It's at the front of the truck,' Ray shouted as their voices moved away from the lowered tailgate.

Harley was sweating – but not just from the heat. 'Qing!' he hissed. 'We gotta go now.'

There was no reply as Harley shoved the heavy blankets off his body, poking and prodding at them to see where the girl had got to. But, of course, she'd already gone and he'd never even heard her leave.

Muttering under his breath, Harley walked as quietly as he could in his sneakered feet down the interior of the truck. He let himself lightly onto the ground, the faint crunch of his soles on the gravel making him flush even hotter with fear. There was no one around the back of the truck. From the tracks in the gravel he could make out that Schumacher had dragged the piano away to the left. From the front of the truck, he could hear his dad insisting, 'Check your computer system – I'm sure the order is in there,' before turning up the truck's radio. The sound of sixties music covered the noises Harley was making as he sneaked away towards the eastern side of the house.

As he crept, Harley studied the face of the grand two-storey, Chinese-style mansion the truck was parked below. There was a set of three wide stone stairs leading up to the recessed front porch of the house which was covered in square, decorative iron panels – nine on each side of the tall, red-painted, double front doors – depicting writhing dragons and phoenixes, horses, tigers and bats, and frightening gods. A stone column carved with dragons and pearls and fruit stood on each side of the giant doors. The walls of the mansion were painted a brilliant white and each of the windows, upstairs and downstairs, was covered in a carved dark wooden window frame in a symmetrical pattern that looked almost like a Chinese character, the carving was so intricate. The roof was covered in shining, narrow, dark green tiles that looked a little bit like pieces of bamboo made out of glazed ceramic. Each corner of the roof curved upwards at the corners, the ridges and roof beams decorated with the sinuous, threatening bodies of ceramic dragons. The uppermost ridge of the roof was also topped with the sinuous, threatening shapes of more dragons.

As the sun beat down on Harley creeping across the grounds below, his eyes darting about for security cameras but not finding any, bright sunlight flared off the eyes of all the watching dragons as if they were made of diamonds.

'They *are* made of diamonds,' Qing hissed as Harley backed into her suddenly.

He almost fell over in fright. It was like she'd literally appeared out of thin air.

'This is the Lair of the Diamond King,' Qing murmured, as she and Harley moved swiftly together around the right side of the mansion into the deep green of the manicured Chinese garden. 'Mo Li Qing's likeness is everywhere.'

Harley barely heard what she was saying as he

surveyed the glorious gardens surrounding the mansion. From where they were standing, the east wing of the house was clearly visible, as was another section of the mansion to the back. The entire building was shaped like a symmetrical cross – if you cut it down the horizontal or the vertical, the two halves of the building would look exactly the same. The landscaped gardens were filled with sweeping lawns and tiled pavilions with the same curving-up roof lines, and there were beautiful bodies of water everywhere, spanned by graceful ornamental bridges. As they crouched down low and ran across the gardens, Harley and Qing passed groves of ancient trees heavy with fruit, and sculpted walks of bamboo and willow. It was the most strange and beautiful garden Harley had ever seen. And it was absolutely deserted.

He looked up into the trees for surveillance cameras so often that Qing snorted.

As they raced around the side of the east wing – which had closely spaced steel bars across all the windows – Qing ran headlong into an old Chinese man in a long-sleeved, navy jacket with a stand-up collar, and loose pants of the same faded colour, who was just rising to his feet from beneath a large peppercorn tree at least a hundred years old.

Although the man looked very frail – his wrinkled skin a nut-brown shade from years spent working in the sun, his hair snow white and cropped close to his head like a Chinese monk – he did not fall over when Qing crashed into him. Instead, he swiftly planted his slippered feet into the soft soil he was standing in, and caught Qing by both forearms. There was a sizzle of static electricity between them, its force pushing the old man backwards. But he somehow absorbed it without flinching, and did not let go of the girl.

She hissed, struggling, and the elderly man let her go immediately, looking sternly at both her and Harley. 'You should not be here,' he said. 'This is private property. I could have you arrested.'

Harley imagined the look on his mother's face and shivered.

'*Nĭn shì shuí?*' Qing challenged the old man as if there were something about him she could not put her finger on.

'I am the gardener,' the old man replied with dignity, indicating the steel hand spade buried in the soil of a flowerbed beside the peppercorn tree. 'And you should not be here.'

'Please, sir,' Harley said politely. 'We just want to see the museum, you know? Just a quick peek. We've come all the way from Australia. It won't take more than a minute.'

The old man blinked, staring at them for a long time: a Chinese girl in antiquated, formal robes, and a Eurasian boy with sticky-up hair, whose knees were coming right through his faded pants. In the buzzing, slumberous garden, the two children were like a strange mirage brought on by the intense morning heat.

When the old man did not speak, Harley insisted, 'It's true!'

The old man seemed to give himself a shake. '*Australia*, you say?' He bent finally, pulling the hand spade out of the ground and straightening slowly. 'All right,' he said. 'But you lead the way. And I have my trusty spade here – in case you try anything funny.'

He waved the hand tool at them to indicate they should start walking and Qing shot Harley a look that clearly said, *I don't trust him.*

Inside his head, Harley replied: *I don't think we have much choice, Qing. At least it will get us inside.*

And Qing nodded as if she'd understood and picked up her pace.

As they opened the steel security door protecting the back entrance to the mansion, which the old man explained was kept unlocked during the day for the ease of the staff, an alarm began to sound somewhere deep inside the grand house. Harley's thoughts flashed to his dad and the CCTV room.

The old gardener said tersely, '*Hurry*. There's not much time once that gets started. Unless it's rung through to the security company as a false alarm, the house will soon be crawling with police.'

The three of them walked quickly through a dark, cool kitchen and laundry quarters that seemed to go on for miles. The rooms they passed were all empty. 'The housekeepers were given a day off,' the old man murmured. 'No one to cook for, you see. They went to stay with family on the East Coast. I have no family – not for a very long time. But I am just one old man. You could not have chosen a better time to visit, children. And from so very far away – it is a long overdue honour.'

As they hurried down the central corridor of the cross-shaped house, Harley gasped in awe. Just at the midpoint of the mansion where the two wings met the front and back sections, there lay a large square fish pond filled with lazily swimming orange and white koi. The internal pond mirrored the shape of an open light well that reached from the ground floor up through the second storey to the sky, illuminating the hollow centre of the house. Harley had never seen a house that had the outside *inside*, and said so.

'Very beautiful,' the old gardener said dismissively. 'The Romans had the same idea. But such a nuisance when it rains. And it's not particularly secure, given the wonders you are about to see. It's amazing no one's ever attempted to take the vase any earlier. I wish they had.'

His tone implied great bitterness. Qing gave the old man a sharp, sidelong look. They had never mentioned any *vase* to him.

Harley gasped again as they reached the edge of the fish pond, the sunlight streaming down where all four sections of the house came together. His dad had been right – just outside the tall, red double doors that led into the east wing, opposite one long edge of the pond, stood a vast stone statue made of different coloured natural marbles and semi-precious stones that reached almost to the ceiling over four metres above their heads. The whites of the fearsome god's eyes appeared to be made of real diamonds, and he wore a Chinese-style warrior's helmet and flowing robes of red and gold and blue. A long black beard and moustache fell down his chest, and he held a tall spear with a curved, golden blade in one hand and a golden sword in the other.

'I've seen him before,' Harley whispered as Qing read aloud the four words carved into the blade of the sword in characters higher than a human hand:

'Earth, water, fire, wind,' the gardener said. 'Yes.'

Harley's face cleared suddenly. 'Antediluvian House!' he exclaimed. 'It's the same god as that statue on the first floor.'

'Mo Li Qing,' Qing reminded Harley grimly. 'As I said, his likeness is everywhere. This was the magician's master. The whole house is dedicated to him.'

Harley's head spun at the coincidence. 'Was he actually *real*?'

The old man looked from Qing to Harley. 'The Diamond King, also known as *Pure*, is the family's personal god and talisman. The Queks are diamond merchants, after all. Their vast fortune was built on their worship of this precious material.' Again his tone was dismissive.

The alarm that sounded from somewhere deep within the other wing of the house suddenly cut off and the silence that followed seemed unnatural.

'Come, children,' the old man urged. 'There is no time to waste. I was once warned that every day I would be tested,' the old gardener murmured this almost to himself, 'but that has proven to be untrue – until, perhaps, today.'

The giant red doors had a huge circle made of iron in the centre, bisected neatly where the doors met. A brass ring wider across than a human head hung down on each half of the iron circle, and there were two empty metal brackets at the top of each semicircle that were clearly meant to hold some kind of horizontal locking bar.

Only the bar was gone.

The old man frowned. 'That's not right!' he exclaimed. 'It is *always* kept locked from the outside when a family member is not within. Someone is already inside.'

Qing stepped forward and placed her hand on the iron ring on the right, intending to pull the door open and go inside.

The old man hissed, 'If you open it, whoever is inside will hear you. It is not kept oiled for that very reason. No one viewing the collection may ever be surprised by an intruder. The entire wing is built like a wooden echo chamber – every footfall is amplified. The acoustics inside are excellent. Sometimes,' the old man's eyes seemed very sad, 'you think you can hear the past speaking directly to you.'

Closing her eyes, Qing bowed her head, her black hair falling around her face, as if she was thinking.

In the space of two heartbeats, Harley watched in horror as she seemed to collapse inwards. For a moment her empty silk robes fluttered through the air, falling towards the floor like leaves, before they, too, seemed to roll in upon themselves and vanish like smoke – and Qing was gone through the crack between the red doors.

Chapter 10

'*Wha—!*' Harley started to exclaim, but the old man put his index finger to his lips for silence and hurried them both behind the vast stone statue of Mo Li Qing. The two of them crouched down behind the base of the statue, listening. Seconds later, they heard a shout from inside.

'I've got to help her,' Harley growled.

The gardener placed a hard, dry, wrinkly hand on Harley's shirtsleeve, his head cocked as if he'd just caught some sound Harley couldn't hear. 'Wait,' he whispered.

At that moment, a man in a khaki security guard's uniform and peaked cap ran past the east wing's doors, the statue, then around the ornamental koi pond. 'Where are you, Captain Jia?' he bellowed into the walkie-talkie he was clutching. 'Wing? Andy? Bong? Fahad? Come in!'

Harley watched as the security guard ran puffing towards the front doors of the house, taking out a set of keys before unlocking the red doors from the inside and throwing them wide open. The guard ran outside, forgetting to lock the doors again in his haste.

There was a crash from inside the east wing and the old man winced. 'Irreplaceable,' he muttered.

'What's going on in there?' Harley wailed under his breath. 'Where's Dad?'

His skin prickled in relief as Ray whispered, 'Right here,' from around the front of the statue.

Harley stood up and moved cautiously around the side of the stone statue so that he was looking up into his dad's face. Ray had lost his grey courier cap and there was a new bruise on his forehead.

'I've disabled the CCTV,' Ray explained hurriedly, 'and Schumacher's temporarily, uh, engaged the undivided attention of the security team. He'll get the one who just ran out the front. We're good to go in. Where's Qing?'

Harley scrunched up his face. 'She's already inside.'

'Great!' Ray grinned. 'Hopefully she's found it already. It's getting hot – and I don't mean the weather. I saw an ice-cream van creeping up the drive a second ago because there's no one at the guardhouse to stop anyone coming in now. And you can bet whoever's in the van isn't here to sell ice-cream. We got in early, but we're going to have company soon. We need to move.'

Ray's expression sharpened as the old gardener emerged from behind the statue, too. 'Who is *he*?' Ray exclaimed.

'He's the gardener,' Harley replied. 'You know, the one who works here? He didn't have family to go to. Qing ran straight into him.'

'That's *bad*,' Ray said, scanning the hallway behind him nervously. 'Apart from security, no one was supposed to be home. Now he's seen you, he's seen me, he's seen her. This is a job for which the word *abort* was invented. We have to split. I'm meant to be a ghost. I've only survived this long because I pretty much leave no trace.'

Ray started to back towards the front doors, waving at Harley to follow.

'Dad!' Harley wailed softly. 'We can't leave!'

'Yes, we can.' Ray's answer was curt. 'You have to tell yourself it's just business – and there will be other opportunities. That way you'll never feel regret.'

'*The girl*,' the gardener reminded Ray quietly, standing with his hands clasped together in front of him, his long sleeve cuffs skimming his knuckles.

Ray stopped dead in his tracks and his shoulders slumped.

'Leave no man behind,' the old gardener said sternly, 'isn't that your motto?'

Ray nodded glumly. 'Even if that man is a kid. Wait a minute, what?' he exclaimed. 'How do you know that?'

'*Especially* if it's a kid,' Harley insisted. 'And we can't leave without that vase. We just can't. We have to help.'

There was a scream from inside, and Ray stood straighter and pushed his shoulders back.

Looking at Ray and Harley with bright eyes, the old gardener placed one tightly closed fist into the palm of his other hand and bowed slightly from the waist at each of them.

'My name is Téng,' the old man murmured.

'You need to promise me that whatever happens, no matter what I do, no matter what I ... look like, you must *destroy the vase*. Do what that girl came here to do. *Promise me.*'

Ray's expression slid into one of shock. 'No,' he said, shaking his head. 'I can't promise that. It's priceless. It's a pre-Song Dynasty vase. We're talking further back than nine-sixty AD! *I* can't destroy it. That's not what I do. And I won't let any of you do that, either.'

'You're a *thief*,' the gardener said shrewdly. 'Why do you care what happens to the things you steal after you steal them?'

'There's ten million dollars at stake here,' Ray almost whined. 'And payment is predicated on there being an intact vase on handover. It's also my only chance to get that price taken off the kids' heads as well.'

'Chiu Chiu Pang wants *your* head, Ray Spark,' the old man whispered, and Ray went white at his words. How did the old man know these things? 'You will never see that money, vase or no vase, and you know it. That money was never meant for you – it was bait. Show up with that vase and you are finished, *and* your son is finished.'

Harley looked from the old man to his dad. 'Is that true, Dad? That you're a *thief*? I'm not a little kid anymore. Everyone's always hinting, but no one ever comes right out and says it. Before we go any further – I need to know.'

A strange, wild look passed across Ray's face like a shadow. 'You can't ever tell Schumacher this,' Harley's eyebrows shot up, because Ray and Schumacher were tighter than real brothers, 'but my motivation for, for… taking things, and I do, I *do* take things, I admit that and I'm very good at it, the best… comes from a different place than greed. You have to believe me.'

Harley looked down at his feet, bitterly disappointed. His mum had been right all along. His dad *was* nothing but a common criminal. And his next action only made Harley's heart lurch even harder inside his chest, if that were possible.

Ray reached inside the breast of his grey jumpsuit and pulled out a small pistol with a fat black grip. 'Don't say anything to your mother,' Ray pleaded as he moved to stand alongside the left door, waving at Harley to hug the hinges of the door on the right side. 'You never saw this in my hand. One day, I swear, I will explain everything.'

Harley shook his head and deliberately looked away from his dad to the old man who was now centring his body before the circular iron door pulls. His feet were planted and his fists rested on each side of his waist, palm sides up.

'*What are you do*—?' Harley began to ask, but the old man suddenly sliced down at the air before him, shooting both his wrists forward so that they were crossed in front of his body.

Then, faster than the Sparks could follow, the old man brought both fists back to chest height and began punching the air repeatedly – first a hard punch followed by a flicking turn of the wrist and withdrawing motion on one side, followed by the exact same action on the other. The closed fist punches changed into bladed hand attacks with the same flicking turn of the wrist, and then multiple rapid palm strikes with the same *flick* and *return* gesture before the old man's open palms began to arc towards the ceiling, first crossing one side of his body, then the other, faster and faster, until his movements and face were a blur of sun-browned skin and dark fabric.

Abruptly, the old man drew both his open palms back towards his chest as if he were readying himself to push something heavy and hissed: '*Kāi!*'

· 152 ·

The tall red doors burst open as if the old man had expelled the north wind from out of his open hands. A man standing halfway down the room with his fingers raised to a glass and black steel pedestal display case actually fell over, as if something huge and unseen had mown him down.

Harley's eyes widened as he took in the length of the east wing in one glance – a long, rectangular chamber with black and white tiled floors and an upper gallery that ran around all four sides, supported by carved wooden columns crawling with dragons painted in brilliant reds, muted greens and gold. There were men brawling all over the upper level gallery and across the ground floor. Some had strange weapons – like the same wicked crescent-shaped blade on a stick that the stone god guarding the door was holding, or long, vicious twin steel hooks with long-handled shafts like butcher's hooks. Other men were switching from western boxing to Chinese boxing, using their fists and legs to become swooping cranes or clawing tigers or leaping eagles in the blink of an eye, before changing styles again, or just trying to headbutt their opponents when none of the fancy stuff would work.

A few of the windows to the outside were open

now, their security bars sheared right through. People were smashing up against or falling across the display cases dotted throughout the room, dangerously rocking the precious artefacts inside. As Harley watched from the open door, his heart in his mouth, a big glazed plate with an intricate ochre and green glazed pattern tipped off its stand and broke into pieces on top of its own pedestal.

Ray groaned as he and Harley scanned the room for any sign of Qing. 'It's killing me to watch this! That had to be early Tang Dynasty, at the very latest.'

'There!' Harley exclaimed, and Ray nodded, having seen the same azure, snake-like flash writhe up one of the dragon columns near the back left corner of the room, moving up and over the banisters into the upstairs gallery.

'I'll cover you, son,' Ray said as they advanced cautiously into the room, no sign of the old gardener anywhere. 'Head for the back left corner staircase, stay low, don't engage; don't *be* engaged. Just like her – you're, uh, smoke. *Move.*'

When a hairless, moustachioed thug in a tight, shiny suit reared up in front of Harley and tried to brain him with an ancient, crescent-shaped shovel,

Ray pushed Harley down onto the ground before Harley could even yell out.

'Uh, uh,' Ray said dangerously, aiming the muzzle of his small pistol between the man's eyes, which widened as he recognised the man holding the gun.

'Мой Бог! Spark's here!' he screamed in a heavy Russian accent. 'Get Spark if you cannot find vase! His head is worth as much!'

The man's voice echoed about the east wing, cutting through the sounds of fists meeting faces and shoes connecting with hardened abdominal muscles everywhere.

Every man in the room seemed to stop what he was doing and turn to look at Ray, who hissed at Harley, 'Now! *Now!* I'll keep them busy.'

Harley rolled to his feet and sprinted for the left staircase at the back of the room as his dad and the thug grappled for control of his pistol. As he ran, Harley caught a flash of brilliant green streaking up the matching staircase to the right.

Harley hugged the back wall as men threw themselves down the staircase next to him, rushing to get a piece of his dad. It was astonishing.

Harley's legs were burning as he made it onto the now deserted upper level. 'Qing?' he called out.

'Here!' she called back, waving from the opposite end of the gallery. 'Someone hid it!'

Qing was standing on an ebony-coloured chair pushed up against the side of a tall, lacquered wooden cabinet which was centred in the space above the doors to the east wing. The open-fronted display cabinet was filled with lumpy earthenware vessels: bowls, plates, vases, urns, ginger jars. All of them were rendered in muddy colours with unsophisticated finishes; they were nothing like the spectacularly coloured examples on temperature-controlled display behind safety glass on the ground floor.

Harley began to run down the gallery towards Qing as she braced herself against the top of the cabinet to reach for a plain brown pot, wide and stumpy and painted with black markings.

Before her fingers could even touch the pot, however, the old gardener was standing at the base of the cabinet, looking up at her. He gave Qing a strange, pained look. 'I can't let you do that,' he murmured. 'I cannot let you have it, much as I yearn to.'

Harley slowed in surprise; he hadn't even seen or heard the old man's approach.

His dad yelled out from below, 'Har-*ley*!'

Harley peered over the banister, shocked to see his dad barely holding off a ring of weapon-wielding men with his shaking gun hand. 'You need to *hurry*, son!'

'Mr Téng?' Harley said, then gave a yell of surprise when the old man turned to look across at him, his eyes glowing a luminous gold, jet-black irises ringed in a thin rim of silvery green. 'What are you doing?'

'Remember!' the old man howled, his face twisting as if lumpen creatures were moving about under his skin. 'No matter what I say, no matter what happens, you must *destroy* it!'

As the old man threw himself onto the ground, twitching and snarling and changing right before their eyes, Qing leant so far around the front of the display cabinet that it began to rock away from the wall. She desperately shoved her left hand inside the top compartment containing the stubby, barrel-shaped jar and caught hold of it with a triumphant cry.

Out of its mouth she pulled a small, familiar-looking vase with a white background and a red potter's mark at its base. Only, this time, the dragon winding around and around the vase was bright…*green*.

Qing slid the ugly pot back into its spot in the cabinet, gazing down at the vase in her right hand, puzzled. She was looking at Harley as if she were about to say something when she was swept straight off her chair – swallowed in the coils of a giant green snake which lifted her off her feet towards the ceiling.

The coils raced up her body until the only parts of her that Harley could see were her face and the hand holding the vase. Qing stared, mesmerised, at the golden eyes of the creature looking fixedly down at her; it wasn't a snake, Harley saw now, but some kind of legless dragon. It had the same ridged and horned head as the green dragon depicted on the vase, and large, rippling green-silver scales – almost like fish scales but plate-sized – and it had no limbs. Its green body was so long and wide that it filled up one whole side of the gallery, and it was floating just above the floorboards.

'*Lǎo fū*,' Qing gasped. 'Let me go. You are a slave to this vase. I can feel it.'

I am bound to it. I have been its guardian – for centuries. The old gardener's voice seemed to speak directly into Harley's head, sounding weirdly amplified, ancient and reptilian, making every hair on the back of Harley's neck stand up. *If you try to take it from me, you will die.*

Dimly, Harley could hear the sounds of men calling out fearfully from below, but the dragon's eyes, and its voice, were hypnotic, and Harley could not look away. The air smelled like tinder, yet it was colder than ice.

The Téng – for that was the kind of creature it was – began tightening its coils around the girl, forced by some long-ago edict to prevent the destruction of the very thing that made it suffer.

'Who is imprisoned in it?' Qing gasped as the coils of the Téng tightened around her. She felt her own nature beginning to change and expand in response, but continued, fiercely, to resist. 'I don't want to hurt you, old one,' she gritted. 'You are kin. You are from my time. You have done nothing wrong except be faithful and steadfast to the safekeeping of this vase.'

It is someone important, like you, the Téng rasped, its tone of despair almost driving Harley to his knees as he stood below the beast's vast, rearing body, Qing struggling high up in its grasp. *That vase contains the beginning of the end. I willingly gave my life to prevent it, but I did not know how long it would be, how long…*

The Téng's wail rose and rose until it seemed it would shatter the roof beams and eaves of the mansion. In it, Harley could sense all the weight of years the Téng had been bound to protect the vase, unable to be truly itself for long, more man now than dragon – dutiful, confused, alone.

'*Aaaaaahhhh,*' Qing cried out as the coils of the Téng bore down crushingly. Her eyes glowed a fierce gold, black irises widening dangerously, and the Téng hissed, drawing its lips back from its sabre-like teeth, cursed to kill any who threatened the vase…

Suddenly, with all her remaining strength and breath, Qing drew her arm sideways with a swift, sharp movement and threw the vase over the banister of the upper gallery.

Nooooooo, the Téng roared, instantly releasing Qing, who fell to the ground and lay there, stunned. Snapping and uncoiling like a taut streamer, the Téng followed the vase over the bannister.

But it could not catch the ancient ceramic vessel before it shattered on the black and white tiles, filling the whole room with brilliant, searing light.

For one moment, Harley thought he saw a tall, broad-shouldered, muscular young man kneeling in the wreckage of the vase. He appeared only a few years older than Harley himself. His black hair was tied tightly into a topknot, and he wore dark leggings, a heavily embroidered green and gold ceremonial surcoat with a coat of pieced-bronze armour fitted snugly over the top. But then with a glare of hatred at all around him and an inhuman leap, the young man was gone, and there was the sense of something emerald-coloured, vast and furious, rushing through the room like an arctic wind before it swooped through the open doors of the east wing and up through the skywell at the centre of the house.

Harley heard the half-blinded men below claw and bellow and scatter as the Téng landed among them in a tangle of loops and coils and claws. Some scrambled out through the open front doors of the mansion, others jumped out of the windows they'd first come through wielding boltcutters and diamond saws.

Half-blind himself, Harley yelled, 'Dad!'

'Here!' Ray called out weakly, trapped between heavy folds of the Téng's coiled body. He'd lost his pistol and was lying on his back on the floor, unable to move.

The Téng looked down into Ray's face, its breath hot upon his skin, and Ray's expression said everything – that he should have believed Harley's story in the first place; that he really wanted to live to see Harley grow up, but that that would probably not be possible now.

'Please!' Harley begged, looking down from the upper gallery as the Téng reared over his father, poised to strike. 'He might be a bad man, but I love him.'

The Téng looked up at Qing and Harley looking down on him from the gallery above.

We have no fight, little sister, little brother, he said, and the Téng's voice in their heads was joyous. *I am free! But look no further for the Children of the Dragon or it* will *be the beginning of the end. That much I know.*

Then the coils of the Téng slid and shifted, and its dragon-like head lifted towards the open doors. With a slither and a bound, it, too, was up and through the skywell in the great mansion on

Balestier Road, like a streak of silver-green lightning lost to sight in a moment.

Harley and Qing stared at each other in awe before looking back down at Ray on the ground.

'You two!' Ray pointed at both of them weakly from where he still lay, flat on his back. 'Take the stairs! *Schumacher!*'

When Harley and Qing finally reached Harley's dad – stepping gingerly through toppled display cases and hastily discarded modern and ancient weaponry to reach him – Schumacher was scooping Ray tenderly off the ground like a little kid. He set his boss back on his feet before dusting off the shoulders of Ray's jumpsuit. Schumacher grinned at Harley and Qing over Ray's head and his eyes were smiling, but Harley could see the tension in them. 'Now we make like the bananas and split, *ja*?' Schumacher reminded Ray of one of his favourite sayings. 'If Interpol don't know you are here, boss, they very soon will.'

Ray held up his hand like a stop sign and turned to Qing. 'What do we do now?' he said urgently, indicating the now blank white pieces of shattered vase that the green dragon had left in its furious wake. 'The vase is hopelessly smashed and there's still a price on your heads, plus I was almost crushed to death by the great, suffocating weight of an apparently mythical creature. When he touched me it felt like, like,' Ray's face showed his puzzled wonderment, '*eternity*. It felt older than anything I've ever taken before from any museum in the world.'

'Harley told the truth,' Qing admonished him.

Ray nodded miserably. 'Everything I've worked for is in jeopardy,' he whispered. 'I'm supposed to be a "ghost", remember? And leave no trace. This is probably the worst day of my professional life. But for the first time in possibly ever, maybe it doesn't matter anymore. What matters is getting you both back to where you belong.'

'Bet this is a mystery greater than any security system you've ever had to crack, right, Dad?' Harley said stiffly.

His dad nodded. 'Solving mysteries is a huge part of what I do…'

'…While running a major criminal empire,' Harley finished for him, still hurt at Ray's earlier revelations.

Ray didn't deny this but hung his head and murmured, 'So where to now?'

Qing's finely arched brows drew together as she stared through the open doors at the skywell through which the brilliant green dragon from the broken vase had vanished. 'The Forbidden City,' she murmured with a troubled look on her face. 'He will go there. To try to locate the other vases. We must stop him before he ...' she closed her eyes momentarily, '... destroys them.'

Ray raised his head at her words. If there were other vases, maybe he could still square things with Chiu Chiu Pang. He would work out the details later, on the fly, like he always did.

'Right then,' Ray said briskly, rubbing his hands together and turning to Schumacher. 'The Forbidden City it is. Radio ahead and tell the pilots to refuel for Beijing. Harls, you're staying with me. It's too dangerous to take you home yet.'

Though he was still mad at his dad, Harley's ears pricked up at the idea of more 'camping'.

Qing turned away from the skywell and searched Ray's face with her eyes, the ring of colour around her dark irises startlingly blue. 'Not Beijing,' she chided gently. 'The Forbidden City of the highest peak of the *Wǔdāng shān* – the Wudang Mountains. In his state of pain and confusion, Tái would have gone home to find answers. I would have done the same in his place.'

Ray's gaze flicked to his son in surprise, then back to Qing. 'You *know* who he is?'

Qing nodded solemnly. 'Táifēng,' she replied. 'The Second Son of the Second Dragon.'

'The same Second Dragon who wanted you and your sisters *dead*?' Harley exclaimed.

Qing nodded again. 'Táifēng, like his father, has always craved power. He will not stop until we are all gone.'

Harley swallowed as she added, 'He's gone to find Master Jìn, the magician who did this to us – to him. We need to find the master, and my sisters, before Tái does – or something very bad will happen.'

Harley's eyes went wide as Qing added quietly, 'In a war between dragons, there are no survivors.'

Chapter 11

After Qing, Harley, Ray and Schumacher re-boarded their private jet and everyone had had a turn in the sumptuous bathroom featuring the full-sized spa with real gold taps, they convened around the boardroom table.

By then, their plane was somewhere over northern Malaysia, bound for a private hangar at Wuhan Tianhe International Airport in China. Qing was retelling the story of the scroll in Garstang J. Runyon's possession at Antediluvian House to a fascinated Schumacher. Ray was listening intently this time, a look of wonderment battling a look of scepticism on his face.

'So you are like the *prinzessen* of the dragon peoples?' Schumacher mused, handing Qing a freshly opened can of sandwich tuna and a small cocktail fork.

'There were many dragon kings across many regions,' Qing replied modestly between forkfuls of tuna. 'Our misfortune is that my uncle never accepted my father's rule.'

At that moment, there was an urgent series of complicated-sounding knocks on the cockpit door from the pilot side. Ray and Schumacher shot upright in their seats as the exact sequence of strange sounds was repeated again.

'*Kinder*,' Schumacher said tersely. 'Bathroom. Inside. *Now*.'

Harley and Qing shot across to the bathroom, leaving the door slightly open. From there, they had a restricted view of the back of Ray's head and couldn't see Schumacher at all.

'Come in!' Ray called out.

Qing and Harley heard a series of locks disengage before one of the co-pilots emerged from the cockpit. They heard Ray say, 'You can uncover your eyes, Withers, it's only me and Schuey in here,' and then they heard the reply, in a crisp English accent,

'Yes, yes, I can see that it's only two grown men and an open can of tuna in here, *which is entirely consistent with the number of persons on our flight manifest.*' The co-pilot said these words extra loudly, as if he wanted to be heard by people possibly secreted in the bathroom.

From their hiding place, Harley and Qing saw the co-pilot step forward into their line of vision, shooting a quick look at the slightly open bathroom door in the process.

'This is not the protocol!' Schumacher replied sternly. 'You are flying, we are relaxing. That is always the way.'

'We're getting messages from certain friendly elements of ground control, sir,' the co-pilot said nervously. 'We understand that, ah, Grandmaster Pang has a large contingent of men stationed at Wuhan Tianhe International Airport to intercept you immediately on arrival.'

Ray leant back in his chair, exhaling loudly. 'Withers, we expressly chose Wuhan Tianhe over Shiyan Wudangshan Airport – which is the closest airport to the mountains – because Wuhan is almost five hours away and was supposed to give us an element of surprise!'

'Grandmaster Pang was tipped off when your flight plan was filed, sir,' the co-pilot responded. 'We're not sure how. We're also told he has men waiting for you at all other airports with private jet facilities in the Hubei, Sichuan, Hunan, Jiangxi, Shaanxi, Henan and Anhui provinces.'

'So we land in Shanghai,' Schumacher replied. 'Only twelve hours by car. No one sees us coming and *boom* – we are there.'

'Chiu Chiu Pang calls Shanghai home,' Ray said dryly. 'If we fart in Shanghai, he'll know about it.'

'*Merde*,' Schumacher replied glumly.

'And he's put a new bounty on your head, Mr Spark,' the co-pilot added, 'which is double the collective bounty for the, ah, children who are not here on this flight with you.'

'Double *merde*,' Schumacher muttered.

'Twenty million dollars?' Ray exclaimed. 'Just for me alone?'

The co-pilot nodded. 'Apparently every master criminal in the world is now on the lookout for you, sir. May I suggest that the, ah, group make an emergency landing on Macau Island instead, taking a night ferry to Hong Kong from where you might hope to slip into mainland China unnoticed?'

'That's almost two days of extra travel time!' Ray exclaimed.

'You should do it, boss,' Schumacher insisted. 'That's an extra two days you get to keep your head.'

'He has a point, sir,' Withers agreed.

Ray turned and looked at the gap in the bathroom door, meeting Harley's worried eye, and sighed loudly. 'Macau it is.'

'A wise choice, sir,' Withers responded, shooting the bathroom door another anxious glance before moving out of the children's line of sight, re-entering the cockpit and re-engaging all the locks.

Harley and Qing came out of the bathroom, Harley's special phone already in his hand.

'Dial your mum, Harls,' Ray groaned, rubbing his face with his hands.

Harley pulled up *Mum* on his contact list and everyone winced as she screeched, *'Ray Patrick Spark!'* to the accompanying sound of Qing's laughter.

CHILDREN OF THE

DRAGON

THE RACE FOR THE RED DRAGON

REBECCA LIM

Read on for a sneak peek
of the next book in this series!

Chapter 1

Harley Spark, thirteen years and twenty-two days old, found himself rapidly descending towards a runway on Taipa Island, Macau, in a private jet with solid gold bathroom taps, in the dead of night. This was all thanks to an ancient dragon vase bearing a rare potter's mark, and a diabolical international crime network of which his dad was an (unconfirmed) member.

Harley's dad, Ray, who should have had his seatbelt securely fastened by now, was pacing up and down, placing a series of increasingly frantic calls in a language Harley couldn't understand. Seated around Harley at the huge meeting table that took up almost the entire inside of the plane were Schumacher – his dad's enormously tall friend and 'helper' (Harley had never been exactly sure what he 'helped' with) – and a mysterious girl called Qing, who was finishing her seventh straight can of sandwich tuna with a cocktail fork.

When she wasn't busy kung fu-ing adult-sized exponents of the Northern Praying Mantis style of Chinese martial art into submission, Qing was usually found eating fish.

'She can really put away the tuna!' Schumacher said admiringly over the sound of the landing gear extending for the final approach.

Qing shrugged and airily opened her eighth can.

Harley studied the chewing girl as the ground rushed up to meet them. She was about his height, with straight black hair severely parted at the centre and hanging down just below her narrow, bony shoulders. She had a serious, triangular face with high, pronounced cheekbones and a wide mouth. There were two things that stopped her looking like any other kid that went to his school. The first was the way she was dressed: in a collarless, tightly belted black tunic crawling with the looping bodies of six coiled dragons embroidered in azure and gold, worn over the top of a floor-length gold skirt and black cloth slippers embroidered with azure and gold dragons. And the second were her eyes: jet black apart from a thin ring of blue, and whites that weren't actually white, but the faintest bit *golden*.

Qing could also – although Harley tried not to think about this too much – apparently move things without actually touching them, and jump off tall buildings without much bother. And it was possible she'd been trapped inside a ceramic vase for over two thousand years, but – out of a sense of extreme politeness, maybe – no one was talking about that part.

As the plane's wheels hit the ground and hurtled to a stop down the runway, not a muscle in the girl's face moved, although she briefly touched the large, almost translucent pearl that she wore on a simple ribbon around her neck, as if for luck.

After they landed, the private jet taxied around to a hangar that was largely shrouded in darkness and well away from the main complex. They disembarked into a dimly lit, echoing space and were met by … nobody.

'He's not here!' Ray Spark hissed in frustration, the outline of the jet looming above him.

'You should have called him directly,' Schumacher muttered, peering out through the open hangar doors. 'There were too many middlemans for my liking, Boss.'

'The *middlemans* are the only way to reach this guy,' Ray whispered back. 'He's deadly with a cleaver and is a fiendishly good getaway driver, but the man refuses to carry a phone.'

Suddenly, Qing inexplicably exclaimed from behind them, 'Prawns.'

A large man in baggy tracksuit pants and a singlet lumbered – silently – out of the darkness. It was as though he'd materialised out of thin air – all two hundred-plus kilograms of him. He did, indeed, smell of prawns and his arms were as big as Christmas hams.

'Spark,' the shadowy man-mountain said, cracking his knuckles ominously.

His silhouette suddenly stood to attention, and Harley wondered why until he noticed that Qing had drifted out from behind Schumacher to study their getaway driver more closely. Harley saw his dad and Schumacher freeze, too, out of the corner of his eye, because it was obvious to everyone present – even the two pilots busily pretending they couldn't see what was going on outside the plane – that Qing was faintly…glowing. She was the only person in the place who was clearly and eerily visible and, as she moved closer to the man who smelled like prawns, it was apparent that the man's singlet was incredibly stained with prawn goo and that he was terrified.

'*Guǐ*,' he breathed, backing away, shaking his head and frantically waving his hands in a *shoo, shoo* gesture.

Ray looked at the man and snapped, 'Ghost? What ghost?'

At Ray's words, what glow there was went out, and Harley had to suppress a yell – for Qing had inexplicably vanished. She just wasn't there anymore. And all he'd felt was a faint draught moving past him.

'You're seeing things, Happy,' Ray added coolly. 'Been working too hard. There's no one here except Schumacher, me and my boy. Let's get going. The longer we delay, the hotter it gets.'

The big man – who looked the opposite of the English name his mum had given him – cast around fruitlessly in the dark for a while, muttering about ghosts, before he led them moodily out to a battered white delivery van with *Hai Tong Tai Seafood Co.* painted on the side in red letters.

The windows in the rear doors of the van were painted over.

'Get in,' Happy indicated with a jerk of his head. He rubbed his bare arms for a moment, as if he were cold – or maybe as if he were smoothing down the little hairs on his skin that were standing up in fright – before moving around to the driver's door and starting the engine. Schumacher, Ray and Harley piled into the pitch-black interior of the van before Happy came back and shut the rear doors with a soft clang behind them. The smell of fish guts in the delivery van was overwhelming.

Ray said, 'Pull up a crate, gents – it's going to be a bumpy ride to downtown Macau.'

Harley was glad that the driver's compartment was closed off from the cargo area because even Schumacher yelled and jumped, hitting his head on the ceiling of the van, when Qing reappeared without warning.

She had a broad grin on her face as she waved a raw fish fillet at them with a faintly glowing hand, then took a delicate bite.

To be continued in **The Race for the Red Dragon**

Acknowledgements

With thanks to my husband, Michael, real-life martial arts action hero, and our fearless and funny kids, Oscar, Leni and Yve, who put up with me walking into furniture and burning the chops when I'm thinking about character and plot. And a huge *vielen dank* to my new brother-in-law, Stefan Kachel, for double-checking Schumacher's German is spot-on.

Huge thanks also to Eva Mills and Jodie Webster, publishers extraordinaire and beloved industry heavy-weights, to my brilliant friend and editor Hilary Reynolds for tidying up all the dangling modifiers and POV issues and listening to me whinge, and to my extended dumpling-loving family at Allen & Unwin, whom I've been privileged to work with, eat with and bounce ideas off for over a decade now.

Having only ever attained an orange belt in Wing Chun Kung Fu, I owe a great debt of gratitude to Lu Shengli's most excellent *Combat Techniques of Taiji, Xingyi, and Bagua: Principles and Practices of Internal Martial Arts* (translated and edited by Zhang Yun and Susan Darley, Blue Snake Books, 2006) and years of watching wuxia movies featuring improbable hairstyles and death-defying stunts.

This is a work of fiction. All of the names, characters, descriptions and events in this book are entirely fictional. Any errors are entirely mine.